Mercury Out Cold

Steve Rzasa

Books

Urban Fantasy
> *Mercury On Guard*
> *Mercury For Hire*
> *Mercury At Risk*
> *Mercury Is Hot*
> *Mercury Out Cold*

Space Opera
> *The Word Reclaimed: The Face of the Deep 1.0*
> *The Word Unleashed: The Face of the Deep 2.0*
> *Broken Sight: The Face of the Deep 2.5*
> *The Word Endangered: The Face of the Deep 3.0*
> *Severed Signals*
> *Cryptic Commands*
> *Failed Frequencies*
> *Mixed Messages*
> *Empire's Rift: A Takamo Universe Novel*
> *Strife's Cost: A Takamo Universe Novel*

Science-Fiction
> *Man Behind the Wheel*
> *Multiverse*
> *For Us Humans*
> *The Echo Watch*

Superhero
> *Airfoil: Origins*

Fantasy
> *The Bloodheart*
> *The Lightningfall*
> *Just Dumb Enough (contributor & editor)*

Steampunk
> *Crosswind: The First Sark Brothers Tale*
> *Sandstorm: The Second Sark Brothers Tale*

CHAPTER ONE

December

I had the pulsar stave ignited, ready to beat back a slavering astral fiend when it …

Kidding.

It was totally dead in my apartment. The only thing battering down my windows was the rain outside. Gloomy clouds shrouded San Camillo's buildings in a sticky fog. Sticky and *cold*. Just another beautiful December.

The pulsar stave was deployed but not powered—not yet. A flicker of will extended through my fingers sent yellow-white energies along its carvings, delivering just enough heat to its target. Said stave flicked a slice of pepperoni off the pie slumped against the inside of a white cardboard box from Carlito's. Warmed it nicely. To be fair to the box, its molecular makeup wasn't much different than the grease soaking its base, so it was probably more pizza than container.

I tossed the slice into my mouth and chased it down with pop. I burped, then let out a contented sigh. Which nobody could hear, because I was on my own. Just me and *The Mandalorian*.

"Yeah, living the dream," I said to the empty apartment.

I twisted on the couch, hoodie and blue jeans barely warm enough. Should've kicked on the heat. Forget that. No way. The forecast said it was supposed to be sunny and low 60s. Not this rainy and 40 crap.

Great. I sighed. Baby Yoda was cute and all, but even he couldn't banish my gloom. If there were literal doldrums, the city was stuck in them. And it was only noon.

My phone perched on the arm of the couch, brushing against my hair when I stretched and yawned for the 95th time that afternoon. Man. Had I even left the apartment? Never mind that. Had I left the *cushion*?

Biggest question: Since when did I care?

Boy. Save the world a couple of times and one's sense of carefreeness gets easily supplanted by responsibility. What a drag.

Enough of that. I punched the speed dial icon at the top of my phone. It rang twice.

"Hello?"

"Hey, Liz."

"Oh, hi, Mercury!" Elizabeth Stojan's voice could have shot a beam of light from my phone's screen, it was so sunny. I pictured her in—ironically—the darkest room of Procyon Foundation's temporary secret headquarters, pink hair catching the glow from dozens of display screens ranging from tiny to huge. "Nice day outside?"

"No, Liz, it's raining. Miserable."

"Oh, yeah? I couldn't tell since we're down here below the silo but I always like to imagine it's pretty out because otherwise it just makes the day dreary and slows me down and then I can't get *anything* done, which is bad because if Ms. Lark—"

"Got it, Liz. Say, since you're hanging out in Tracking, could you—"

"Nope."

I blinked. "Nope? Nope, what?"

"Nope, as in, no tachyon spikes, no interdimensional rifts, not a single rip in the past three weeks, or any other readings out of the ordinary."

"Okay. You auditioning for Forecasting? I thought they were fresh out of dreamers to tell us when astral fiends might next make their appearances."

"No, um, but this is like the sixth time you've called me since Tuesday."

Tuesday? I craned a neck. There was one of those freebie nature calendars stuck to the fridge, this year's featuring coastal California photos. December was a nighttime image of San Camillo's skyline glittering across the bay. Yikes. It was Saturday. And me, without plans. I mean, without plans beside epic *Star Wars*.

"Still there, Mercury?"

"Yeah, I'm here. I figured I'd check. It's quiet

around here." Especially with Loredana gone. She and her girlfriends had headed Los Angeles for a ladies' weekend. Good timing.

We were getting married in twelve days.

I glanced at my stealth suit. Gray and black patterns fit together like puzzle pieces, glistening in the lamplight. I should be off the couch, fighting crime. Seriously. With the near end of the world a few months before and the almost-immolation of San Camillo not long after, I'd kind of let the whole local vigilantism thing slide. I mean, I'd charged for the work because hey, I needed the money, but since I'd been back in Procyon's good graces, I didn't require extra income.

Not a great reason for taking a break, I know.

I checked my phone. Yeah, the public had noticed. People griped about me not preventing the things police had to clean up after—all the ravages of a big city. But keeping everything this side of the Interstice dimension safe from astral fiends who'd love nothing better than to drain humans of their lives took priority.

Maybe it was time to branch out, though. As in, the real hero stuff.

"Okay. So, let's do it." I slapped my hands on my knees and launched upright. And immediately grimaced, thanks to the dull ache in my leg that turned into a full-fledged stabbing pain. My prosthetic held my balance nicely, but the stump where flesh and blood ended still hurt. Bad weather made it throb worse.

I grabbed the suit. Shimmied out of my jeans and into the form-fitting attire. The pulsar stave's energies writhed across its surface and bled into the suit, which channeled them into—well, channels, I guess. Bright lines on the jumpsuit's borders. The stave's energies also filtered into the prosthetic leg, which Liz had built along the same technology as my outfit. Lent me a nice boost if necessary.

I checked myself out in the mirror and grinned. "Not too shabby."

So, Liz didn't have any monster for me to chase, huh? No problem. I could find bad guys aplenty. I banged open the living room window and leap onto the fire escape …

Right. Still raining.

The cold downpour hadn't let up. I let water run off my face a moment before concealing all my features with the suit's mask. "Seriously?"

Well, good thing the suit's feet were fabricated with traction in mind. They stuck like magnets to the slippery metal as I vaulted down the fire escape and across to the next building.

Yeah, I know—dumb move, leaving my apartment that way. The suit had a bonus, though: Invisibility. Or, better put, adaptive camouflage. I was a blur of asphalt, brick, glass, and clouds as far as anybody who glanced out their window was concerned.

Ready to rock. Ready to put the smack on bad guys in my neighborhood.

And after thirty seconds perched on the railing, the rain managing to dampen me even through the supersuit, I took another look out the cars splashing through the puddles past lampposts sporting soggy wreaths and muttered, "Forget this."

I went back in and shut the window. What was my major malfunction? It's like I was tangled up in astral fiend's tentacles, except pizza and beer and TV were threatening to drain my life away. I yanked the mask down and rubbed my face. Get a grip, Mercury.

Gee, it was almost like some major event had me anxious.

Wedding, maybe?

Spoiler: I'd never been to one. Not even someone else's. So, the thought of standing up in front of people with Loredana before me, in the dress she still wouldn't reveal …

Fear's not a word I throw around lightly.

My phone buzzed. Fingers crossed—Liz? No such luck.

Instead the caller ID told me I was getting Lieutenant Gabriel Ramos, San Camillo Police Department. Joy. I answered, "Yo."

"Will you stop? You sound like you're auditioning for an MTV special." Ramos had one of those voices that made him sound like he was perpetually perturbed—which, in fairness, he was. And I may or may not have had something to do with that on more than one occasion. "Suit up and get out to Court Street, by the overpass."

"MTV special? Look, Ramos, if you're gonna insist on talking like a forty-something I'll have to up my game for snarky rejoinders."

Ramos sighed. I swore I could feel the breeze. "Just hurry up, will you? This one is right up your alley and I didn't want to call out the rest of the task force."

Task force? As in San Camillo Police Department Extraordinary Crimes Task Force? Whew. Clunky acronym aside, I was all about putting in some mileage with the SCPDECTF—or goon squad, as we liked to call it. "On my way. Don't slay any monsters before I show up."

"Wouldn't dream of it." He hung up the call.

And I had already flung myself through the rain to the next building.

Court Street's neighborhood didn't look any better in the rain. But it smelled less terrible, because of the trash getting flushed down the gutters. I mean, sure, the electric candles in scattered windows and the one plastic Christmas tree put up a valiant fight against the blahs. Gloomy weather made the ramshackle buildings and pockmarked asphalt more depressing. Bonus? No drug dealers hanging out on the street corners. Even they stuck to indoors.

I somersaulted off a rooftop, did a parkour bounce twice down the sides of it and its neighbor, and thumped atop a Dumpster without slipping.

Heck of a superhero landing.

Too bad the only person to appreciate it was Ramos.

He crouched behind the same Dumpster, his semi-automatic pistol drawn. Huh. He didn't have his rifle, so it must be an astral fiend of the smaller variety. Funny Liz hadn't spotted it—but given the way Procyon reorganized its secret activities, I wasn't surprised they'd missed a rip and the accompanying fiend's entry. "Hey, Ramos."

"Get down here!" Ramos wore a SCPD ballcap and a navy-blue jacket with the same insignia on the back. He had rubber boots on over his shoes, which if you'd ever seen his fancy Oxfords, you wouldn't mock. A white collar peeked from under his jacket, plus the top of a black tie. Spiffy as always. "Stay out of sight."

"What gives?" I splashed next to him. Mud spattered his coat.

Ramos grimaced and wiped it off. "I had a call we were supposed to show up at this location."

"Oh yeah? Liz tip you off?"

"It's not that simple." He chewed his lip, as if he were a 10-year-old boy afraid his dad was gonna find out a baseball broke the living room window. Ramos, nervous? What kind of bizarre day was this? "Here it comes."

No kidding. Rain that had been falling straight down swept into a mini typhoon, swirling a few feet in from the mouth of the alley. Light exploded from its center, expanding into a glowing sphere.

"I'm on it!" I willed power to the pulsar stave and broke it in half, wielding each one like a short dagger. Their energies coursed through the suit and soaked my cells. Man, I felt like I could have run from San Camillo across a couple time zones to the Mississippi River. I blasted for the newborn portal.

The raindrops slowed, frozen like jewels as I accelerated across the couple dozen feet to the portal. Cracked me up, when I moved fast and everything went like molasses, because even Ramos' shouted warning became a low-octave, distorted parody of the real deal.

Whatever was coming through the portal, I was gonna plant the pulsar stave clean through its ugly face.

It wasn't until the portal's writhing light show coalesced into a decidedly non-monster form that I realized, duh, the rips that spat out astral fiends were ringed with purple lightning and dark as night, whereas this thing was a glowing soap bubble that had just popped.

Too late. My arms were in motion, slashing through the air with blazing beams of yellow-white extradimensional energies.

"Mercury!"

I broke left, hurling myself aside before I straight-up slaughtered Dominic Zein, the guy diving out of his own portal. He slid sideways in a move I'd have expected of a trained ninja, not an architect.

Fortunately, blasts of blazing light from the shimmering wristbands he wore helped knock me off course.

Unfortunately, they had the side effect of slamming me bodily into a brick wall. I rebounded and ended the heroic charge on my back.

"Ow," I said. Seemed appropriate.

Dominic's face appeared upside down over mine, glowering with all his teeth—wait a second. Upside down. The jerk was *grinning*. "I told you surprising him would be a great idea, Lieutenant."

Ramos holstered his gun. He stood there, hands on his hips, shaking his head like your average disappointed assistant principal looking for the next punk kid to drag to detention. "We could have just messaged him."

"But he likes things with style, with flair. Right, Mercury?" Dominic moved aside and offered me a hand. I let him help drag me upright.

"Yeah. Super fun." My head throbbed. A quick touch and my fingers came away with a streak of blood. No biggie. I'd heal up inside of the next fifteen minutes, especially with all the energies flowing from the stave through me and the suit. "This your guys' idea of a practical joke? Watching me turn Dominic into a human kebab?"

"Don't say that. Kebab." I heard a gurgling; Dominic rubbed his stomach. Dude was wearing black slacks, nice shoes, and a white shirt with black tie. Just like Ramos. "I'm famished. Let's get out of the weather."

"I might have left that part out of our communication." Ramos smirked.

"Hey, kids." I pointed with both staves at my chest. "Here's me, still not finding this funny, and still getting soaked."

Dominic sighed. "This is what I get for being spontaneous."

"Except you just said it was your big plan. For what, exactly?"

He scowled and pointed his wristbands at us. The Echo Watches, handy devices for teleporting from Point A to Point B on Earth and also to myriad other worlds—like Meda, which was my home dimension, or the alternate Earth that Dominic had visited to track his evil twin. Both long stories. But good ones.

The portal swept us up in dizzying spin of zero gravity and darkness. I thought I might die. Which, in fairness, I thought would happen every time we teleported. Before I did, though, the portal dumped us out on the wood floor of a warm and blessedly dry loft apartment.

Ramos staggered back onto a couch. "This had better get easier if we're using the same mode of transportation all night."

"It will. Relax." Dominic doffed his jacket and brushed at thick black hair. The guy looked like a Middle Eastern movie star, slim face and dark eyes. The suit jacket underneath completed the picture.

Hang on. Ramos was wearing a blazer, too.

I dragged the supersuit's mask off and glanced at them. "*Men in Black* marathon? Because I gotta say, not my favorite movie."

"If this is the attitude he exhibited during your encounter, I would surmise the revelation was not received with great mirth."

Hold up. Teget? Yeah, the young guy of mixed Asian-and-other descent lounging on a second couch, warming his hands by the fireplace. I was used to the smile on his face, framed by a neatly trimmed goatee and moustache, but I was not used to him dressing up like a third member of the Blues Brothers. He preferred loose-fitting padded armor and leather, manufactured on Meda, in our home dimension. The sleek wool trenchcoat made him look even cooler.

"Guys, c'mon. Why's my brother dressed like—" I waved my hands around. "Like all of you?"

The door to the loft—Dominic's, I recognized— opened. A tall, broad-shouldered redheaded man in his late thirties came in with a garment bag slung over his shoulder. Blue eyes targeted me, and he chuckled. Brandon Tusk: Flying superhero from Drake City on the other side of the USA. "You got him? Nice."

"Hey, Brandon."

"Hey, yourself. Sorry I'm late, gang. I had to pick this up from the Procyon office. The Rampart manager insisted Ms. Lark left it for Mercury and ..." He let go of the garment bag. It flew twenty feet across the room. I snagged it by its hook with one finger. "Your size, Mercury."

"Brandon ..." I massaged my forehead. Yep, headache. From brick wall impact or annoyance? Take your pick. Because flaunting our powers in mixed company was generally a bad idea. "Ramos isn't in on the team roster."

"Oh." Brandon winced. "I'd assumed you'd told him our identities."

"He hadn't." Ramos was staring at him, but not in fear. At least, he didn't seem scared, or even amazed. "Don't worry. I assumed you were the one called Airfoil."

"A gifted investigator," Teget said to Dominic.

"I'm that, yes, but it's down to process of elimination." Ramos held up three fingers. "Three of you stop the Hedron of Orbits from destroying San Camillo. Two of you were sloppy with masks, and I was right there in the action, getting a good look. Only one of you kept your face a closely guarded secret—and that one was good at making things fly."

"We might as well put up billboards," I muttered.

"Quit whining, Mercury." Ramos straightened his tie. "Don't be the grump at your bachelor party."

"My *what*?"

"The celebration of your approaching marriage!" Teget bounded from his seat, with way too much enthusiasm. He grabbed me by the shoulders and swung me around. Twice. "Brother! Let us gift to you this evening of merriment!"

"That's me, all about merriment." It dawned on me that my brother, my mentor, and two superheroes from across the country had kidnapped me to Rampart, Colorado for a bachelor party. Using a portal. "Wait, are you serious? My party?"

"Against my better judgment, but, yes." Dominic shrugged. "Figured I could minimize damage if I planned it. So, go get changed and we'll get out of here. Reservations are at 8."

I checked my watch. Still running on Pacific Coast Time even though I'd teleported across the Rocky Mountains. "Um, that's in like seven hours."

Dominic extended his wrist. The Echo Watch separated into a whirl of fragments, and a new portal appeared, this one anchored to a faint stain on the wood floor. Wind whipped at the magazines discarded on a coffee table.

I peered through the light-fringed doorway to— the Eiffel Tower?

"Not in Paris!" Dominic hollered over the roar of wind. "Let's go!"

CHAPTER TWO

on't worry. Dominic was smarter than to beam us right smack into a crowd of tourists at Christmas. One minute, we were in a cozy loft over downtown Rampart, Colorado. The next, we stood under a cluster of trees lining a long park stretching to the Eiffel Tower. Hundreds of white tents spread the entire length, cordoning a gleaming rectangle set aside for ice skaters. Everyone was too busy in their shopping and celebrating to notice us five materializing behind the dark backsides of those tents.

I gazed up at the swooping sculpture of lights. Now *that* was a Christmas present.

"Champ de Mars." Dominic pulled his sleeves down under the Echo Watches. The silvery devices had pulled themselves back together, so they resembled antique bracelets, something an archaeologist would have unearthed.

"And here the farthest from home I've ever been

is Florida," Brandon murmured.

"Seriously?" I elbowed him. "What about our one and only team-up?"

"Okay, you're right. San Camillo, before this." Brandon buttoned his jacket. "And I didn't even have to fly to either."

"*Mi pobre cabeza.*" Ramos massaged his temples. "At least my stomach's settled. If I'm going to enjoy a night out, I had better be able to enjoy the local cuisine."

"This way, guys." Dominic walked backwards, waving at us like he was an air traffic controller. "The restaurant's a couple blocks over and up Rue de la Federation."

"You a regular in France?" I caught up with him.

He grinned. "Sort of. My work for Procyon entails a lot of travel, looking for people with familiar faces."

"And by familiar, you mean exact same faces as people from this dimension."

"Mercury." Teget took me by the arm, his expression way too grave for a guy about to party. "I am newly accustomed to your Procyon clan's operations, but is it not inadvisable to speak of things which the layperson deems to be myth?"

"I'd second that 'inadvisable' part," Brandon said. "Our secrets are important."

"Good luck getting him to stopper that bottle," Ramos muttered, his hands jammed into his pockets. "This is Mercury we're talking about. What is his record, thirty seconds without speaking?"

"Here's hoping he's mute when he sleeps, or Loredana will never get any rest," Dominic said.

Brandon and Ramos chuckled at that. Teget slapped me on the back, hard enough to blow air from my lungs, as he joined in their laughter. My cheeks burned. "Funny guys, really. How about you keep my fiancée out of this."

"Easy. No offense meant."

"Don't worry about it." I grinned back, but it was a phony one.

The others lapsed into conversations that wove around me. Ramos sidled up as I dropped back from the pack. "What's bothering you?"

"What? Nothing. This is cool." I tried on the grin again and spread my arms wide. "I mean, Paris, right?"

"Dominic touched a nerve."

"No."

Ramos made that face that meant he didn't believe me. Other people get a similar expression if they lick an onion. "Don't bother faking. I know you. No witty comeback? Something he said stung. That bit about Loredana …"

"Let's do therapy later." I sniffed the air. "Hold up. That's what I think it is. Sausage. Mozzarella. Dominic, you fiend—you found a French pizza joint!"

"Yes, I did."

We walked right by it.

"Not cool," I sighed.

"Ours is around the corner."

Our entourage crossed a narrow intersection by a nice little café, hedged in by the world's tiniest cars and most diverse collection of scooters. The buildings were all pasty except where red and green Christmas lights lent their glow; Dominic babbled to Brandon about who built what when, and to his credit, our Airfoil seemed fascinated.

My brain had switched over to hungry mode.

The green letters shining under lamps proclaimed "Restaurant Erawan" and the smells, man, the smells told me I'd love the Thai food inside.

Wasn't long after we all crowded around a window table that we'd turned our full glasses of wine into half glasses. Laughter echoed around the spaces as Brandon bragged about tackling his latest bad guy. Bad lady, really.

"Flipped her car right over, midair." He demonstrated with one hand, then angled his other hand in for a landing like it was a jet. "I wanted to make everyone back down, so I peeled the bottom off the car like a sardine can."

Dominic whistled. Teget slapped the table so hard Ramos' glass bounced. He caught it before it could douse his shirt in Merlot. "Property damage is your thing, isn't it?"

"They don't call him Air-foul for nothing," I said, winking.

Dominic and Ramos dissolved into snorts and chuckles. Brandon's cheeks reddened but he shook his head, a smirk curving his lips. "I've got better things to do than poke monster squids with a stick all night."

Teget stood, his finger pointed at my face. "He has wounded you! Retaliate!"

"Easy, easy. It's funny." I wiped tears from the corner of my eyes and dragged him back into his seat. "Hey, I won't be too hard on *Airfoil*, because everybody knows he's got the coolest supersuit out of all of us."

"Armored, too," Brandon said.

"Whatever, flyboy. Pass me the mussels."

The plate clattered among its neighbors. Two mussels, stuffed full of spices and meats and unidentified deliciousness that burned my mouth in a good way rose from one side, wobbled through the air, and skidded through the lamb sauce congealing on my plate.

Brandon had two fingers raised in my direction. His face was pinched in concentration, until the last one landed. Then he exhaled.

Ramos sipped his wine. "Convenient."

"I'd show you how I can warm them up to the perfect temperature, but I don't want to steal Airfoil's thunder." I rolled my eyes. "Maybe Dominic could teleport the food into his stomach?"

Dominic grimaced. "The Echo Watches don't work that way, and I'm hesitant to try anything approaching Brandon's level of fine control. Seems— messy."

Teget tore a chunk of chicken off from the whole bird at our table. His teeth stripped meat from the bone. "In battle, mess can seldom be avoided. I doubt there were many complainers of our 'mess' when we routed the evil forces of the Whisperer and his minions before they could drown Mercury's fair city."

"Drop by the fair city's City Hall some time and I'm sure the mayor could give you an earful," Ramos murmured.

That brought another round of laughter from the guys, but my brain had wandered off, back to Dominic's jibe. Not that he was wrong. I'd zonked out on the couch during one too many episodes of *Dr. Who* that I knew I did talk in my sleep. Loredana had elbowed me awake and relayed the conversation with glee.

But her getting rest? Well, I had no idea.

See, we hadn't … Okay. We made the decision we wouldn't … Was it hot in the restaurant? I sipped some more wine. Ahem. Let's just say, I had no clue what Loredana's bedtime routine was. Not firsthand.

Or anybody else's, for that matter.

I twisted a napkin around my finger. Did that make me a weirdo? I think people assumed, what with how brash I was—that's a Ramos word, "brash"— that I had experience. Guess what? Wrong.

My phone buzzed. Loredana. Her face smiled at me from the contact list, red eyebrow twitched up above a sapphire-blue eye. The text? <I hope you fellows have quite the time on Dominic's whirlwind

tour. Were he any more gleeful, one would have assumed I gave him carte blanche to design an entire city. I love you.>

A photo followed—Loredana up close, beaming, with three women in the background. A brunette, and two Black women, one with long, curly hair and the other with a shorter do. I recognized the latter as an employee of San Camillo's chamber of commerce. The others? Seen them around, a few times. But Loredana was private with their names. Her life away from Procyon was hers. I was thankful to be part of it.

The phone trembled in my hand. I shoved it in my pocket. Did I say I was worried about the wedding? The ceremony itself didn't worry me. Any dope could slap on a tuxedo and talk back to a preacher.

It was the wedding night that made me wish for an astral fiend's attack.

"...Are you with us, Mercury?"

Teget, seated to my left, tapped on my plate. He tapped a little too hard and a mussel shell flew through the air, aiming for a blond woman's head as she howled at her date's joke.

The shell halted in midair, then dropped to the floor.

Brandon winked at us and raised his glass in salute.

"Yeah, yeah, I'm good." I grinned. "What's the plan, Dominic? I'm stuffed like a turkey on the wrong holiday. Back to town? Carlito's, anyone?"

Ramos rolled his eyes but couldn't get rid of his

chuckle. Dominic leaned forward, his whisper so soft I thought he was gonna ask if I knew where the Ark of the Covenant was hidden. "How's your Polish?"

"Um, I'd say I'm fluent in Google Translate."

"Don't eat another bite." He shoved my plate away and stood up. "Gentlemen? This one's on me."

Cheers resounded from our table. Even Ramos raised his credit card with a flourish before stuffing it into his wallet. "As long as I don't have to pick up the bill for the whole night," Brandon said. "I'm on a budget."

"Don't cheap out on me yet." I made a show of checking my watch. "We haven't even hit the ten o'clock mark."

"You try telling a teenager he can't get a new computer because his and his colleagues went out for dinner *in Paris*."

"That snotty secretary of yours?" I made a face. "Tell him to get his act together answering the phone first, and then he'll earn it."

"I am never taking parenting advice from you, ever." Brandon shook his head.

It wasn't until we piled out of the restaurant into the chilly air of late-night Paris that Dominic's weird question stuck in my brain.

"Hang on a sec," I said. "Polish?"

Dominic shook his cuffs loose. Echo Watches, here we come.

⌗ ⌗ ⌗

We materialized by a statue of John III Sobieski. That's who Airfoil—er, Brandon—said the old dude in tarnished bronze was on the horse, who was also bronze.

Dominic led us in a dash across the Targ Drzewny—don't ask about the pronunciation—and into a café-slash-nightclub called Klub Rozsada. The music was jazzy, loud, and reverberating off the walls. Whatever the old warehouse had been, some enterprising soul had converted it into a combination of coffee bar and dance hall. And when I say dance, I'm not talking about a strobe-lit grind-fest. I meant, dancing. Like swing and whatever else folks were fond of in the Twenties.

Ramos secured us a round table with leather couches not far from the coffee and way too close to the dancing. Brandon brought us over cups of a dark and minty concoction with major zing to it.

"Who's got the toast?" He swirled his cup. "Because I've got to work this weekend and there's no way I'll be fit to serve the public if I'm glowering through clenched teeth."

"City hall?" Ramos asked.

"Library. Same reputation, less pay."

Ramos and he clinked cups.

"Let me get this, boys." I raised my mug. "To the dream team—seriously, the best batch of heroes to kick astral fiends and whatever other crazy threats come barreling through this dimension and the next. Thanks for getting me out of a really lousy afternoon, and not making me pay for a plane ticket."

That brought a shout of joy from Teget. We clanked our mugs and, after Ramos was done muttering about spilled coffee on his slacks, my brother embraced me. "Mercury, you are a true warrior and a credit to our bloodline. Our parents would be proud."

Figures he would get all sappy when the vino had been too primo. I put on my best "Aw, shucks," face and blinked a lot. "You're great, too."

He laughed and slapped my back, for what had to be the sixth time that night. Pretty sure I was gonna have a Teget-hand-sized bruise on my shoulder blade in the morning. Then he vanished into the packed crowds of people, all ages, twenties, thirties, ranging up to a few couples who looked they lived through World War II but moved with the skill of ballet students.

I slumped back onto the couch next to Ramos, my shoulder knocking his. I dug out my phone and texted back to Loredana, <Love you too. Have fun out there! Smooch from behind the old Iron Curtain.>

Ramos snorted. "Smooch? You're practically married as it is."

"Keep talking, Ramos. You know you're having fun."

"Like I said, I enjoy a night out like any other person." He drank his coffee, arm over the back of the chair, jacket unbuttoned, same as a dozen other guys lounging around the place while couples and batches of ladies danced to a beat as bright as the lights festooning wrought iron railings along the balconies. I hadn't noticed before—the entire upper floor was a series of balconies and catwalks, leading deeper into the former warehouse.

A lot of people up there. A lot of men, in dark suits. With their hands folded. Standing at attention. Watching. Listening.

Definitely not partying.

"You see them?" Ramos drank more coffee, but his eyes were locked on the balconies like lasers.

"Sure. Bodyguards for oil magnates or tech billionaires. Whoever wants to hang out in jolly Poland." I glanced at my superhero pals. They were watching the catwalks, too, but once Dominic mentioned post-war construction techniques and Brandon questioned the historical accuracy of those techniques, I remembered they were first and foremost an architect and a librarian. As in, dorks.

"Sure. That sounds plausible." Ramos swirled his cup. His cup, I noticed, was empty. Nothing to swirl. He sipped from it one more time. "I'm going to go to the bathroom."

He was gone from the seat before I could grab his sleeve. "Hey! This is my party. Evening out. You're not a cop here."

"I'm a cop everywhere."

"Um, except where you don't have jurisdiction."

"That's true. But I can't overlook things I see. No more than you can go anywhere without that."

He leaned in and tapped the side of my jacket. His fingertip clinked against metal.

Okay, he got me. Just like American Express. Good thing we didn't have to sneak the pulsar stave past TSA. "Fair enough. But c'mon—let me send Teget to poke around. Teget's a warrior and …"

Ramos smirked. "Wayward brother?"

"He is. Apparently." I checked either end of our seats. Then behind us at the coffee bar. Heck, I even looked down by our feet. "Where'd he go? No portals around …"

Still wearing what had become a smile, Ramos pointed to the right.

Because Teget was in the middle of the dance floor, arms around a tall, black-haired woman with whom he—was that a waltz? A tango? A combination of the two, plus extra steps I'd never seen. Clearly something he'd learned on Meda. Not Earth standard.

"How about that." I chuckled. "What do you guys think? Gonna see if you can find a match?"

Dominic's eyes widened. "Wow. He's good. But I'll pass. Jess wouldn't be pleased if someone tagged me on Facebook. And things have been tricky enough."

I raised an eyebrow at Brandon.

"Don't look at me." He grinned. "I've got a girlfriend."

"Well, Ramos, that leaves—"

Yeah, he was gone.

Great. "Hang on, fellas. I'll be right back. Duty calls."

I pushed through throngs of people. No sign of Ramos in the hall to the bathrooms. I checked around a couple corners, and when I craned my neck …

The guys on the balconies were letting a pack of suits and dresses into double doors. Once all were admitted, the doors closed.

Ramos sidled along the wall, in the shadows, until he reached a door that was recessed in an alcove. Potted plants as tall as a golden retriever blocked most of the view, but I saw enough to see that sneaky police lieutenant lean against the door. He found his phone and started talking into it. He laughed, shook his head, and launched into an entertaining story with whoever was on the other end.

Faker. No way that was really Ramos.

Then he opened the door and slipped inside.

"Wonderful," I muttered.

Back at the table, a sweaty version of Teget—sans jacket and tie—flopped onto his seat. "Such an invigorating place! Training for the temple guards does not reach such—"

"Zip it." I jerked a thumb. "Ramos is on to something. Like, criminal."

Brandon was at my side first. Dominic sighed, set his coffee cup down, and straightened his tie. "Trouble?" he asked.

"I'd be disappointed if it wasn't. C'mon, let's check it out." But before Brandon could get moving, I put a hand on his shoulder. "You hang back and pay the bill."

"Why now?"

"Because when we break stuff," I said, stalking toward the stairwell, "I don't want it tallied on our tab."

CHAPTER THREE

I didn't want our quartet barging into whatever Ramos thought he'd discovered. A big group of not-Polish dudes would go a long way toward being conspicuous.

Teget and I went first.

We paused outside the alcove door. Teget stood at attention, just like the presumed goons who'd been watching the big doors earlier. Did a pretty good thug impression, especially since he donned his wool trenchcoat. Must be steaming. Of course, if he'd brought the ax—one of two partner weapons to the pulsar stave—he'd have made an even better guard.

I eased up to the door. The cold metal of the pulsar stave prodded my side. Hang on. If I'd been smart enough to bring along my weapon… "Teget. Are you, uh, carrying?"

Teget lifted open his jacket. Yep, there it was, a triple-bladed ax stuffed under his armpit. It had a short handle, made of a gleaming brass metal imprinted with swirling lines. Each thick, curved blade was set equidistant around the handle, aimed down toward his leg. Don't know where he'd gotten the reverse holster for it, but my money was Garvey in Procyon's armory hooked him up.

"Awesome. Let's peek." I opened the door.

We slipped through onto another dark balcony, this one ringing a warehouse that hadn't seen the benefit of Rozsada's renovations. Dingy floors, rusty posts, crumbling concrete. Made me wistful for the simpler days of last year when all I had to worry about was waiting around for an astral fiend to pop out of a rip through space-time in one of San Camillo's many abandoned buildings.

The ground floor, though, was full of people.

They must have gone down the steps leading from the far end of the catwalks to the bottom level. Two goons blocked the big doors through which the crowd had entered, maybe fifty feet to our left. Teget crouched beside me, eyes watchful, face wary. He pointed to our right.

Ramos hunkered by a metal strut, half-hidden in shadow from our perspective, but with floodlamps blazing at the crowd below, he'd be invisible from their view.

This was a different crowd from the Rozsada's dance floor. Everybody looked like they had money, from the guys in shiny suits and even shinier shoes, sporting gold chains like they were entering a Mr. T fashion show, to the women in gorgeous gowns who were wearing millions of dollars' worth of gems. Everyone had champagne, too, served by a couple pairs of the scrawnier goons. By scrawnier, I mean they were shorter than six feet six.

"What manner of gathering is this?" Teget whispered.

"Beats me. Party behind the party?" Though it wasn't nearly as invigorating as the boisterous music we'd left behind. These folks murmured in tight knots, two or three couples apiece. More guys in suits brought out black and silver boxes to a raised platform at the opposite end of the warehouse. A podium flanked the platform.

Something rustled behind us, the sound as soft as a piece of paper. Teget swung the ax up under Dominic's chin.

I had the pulsar stave deployed, too, but resisted the urge to fire it up since I didn't want to advertise our location. "Geez, guys, a little warning. That's twice now one of us has almost sliced up Dominic in the same day."

Brandon brushed aside the stave and joined me at the railing. "So, who are these people?"

"Don't know. But they're unpacking ... stuff. Can't tell from here." I squinted. "Check out those tattoos on the arms of the ones doing the moving."

Brandon frowned, and then let out a long breath. "Great. Polish mafia."

I snickered. "Wow. That's awesome. What, do they shoot themselves whenever they come after their enemies?"

"I'm serious, Mercury. These are the nastier cousins of the same kind of men who caused havoc in Drake City over the summer. You saw that on the news, right?"

"Sort of. The villain you took out had his own henchmen ..." My eyes widened. "*Them?*"

Brandon nodded.

"Perfect. Wonderful. What a great place for a party." I glared at Dominic. "You want to make yourself useful and get a hold of Ramos before he does something stupid? As in, stupider than the five of us creeping in here?"

Dominic scowled but did as ordered, skulking along the wall to Ramos' position. My favorite SCPD saw him coming and motioned for us all to, uh, get lost.

I shook my head and crooked my finger like I was grandma and little Ramos had gotten caught chasing bunnies with the lawnmower.

Ramos followed Dominic back. "You should have stayed put."

"You should have listened when I said don't play cop!"

"Not playing, Mercury. Investigating."

"Yeah? What's next? We all enroll in Interpol?"

"I have contacts with them in Belgium and the Czech Republic."

I rolled my eyes. "Of course you do."

"Hey." Dominic waved his hands between us.

"Time out. Look down there."

A stocky man in a silver suit jacket worn over black shirt and pants took to the podium. His hair was spiked so blond he could have taken grooming tips from Billy Idol. When he spoke, I thought I was listening to the extras cast in *The Hunt for Red October*. "Good evening, all. Welcome back for the second half of our auction. This next lot is ancient Macedonian, recently … liberated from a private collection the Aegean. Bidding will start at eight thousand euros."

And right off the bat, hands shot up. Each one held a tiny white sign with black numbers.

The auctioneer's voice accelerated, devolving into—of all things—a Texas drawl.

"That's weird," Brandon murmured.

"He must have gone to auctioneering college in the western United States," Dominic said.

The three of us who'd grown up in this dimension stared at him.

"What? There are such places." Dominic shifted his crouch. "I looked at it once, before I settled on architecture."

"Black market art," Ramos said. "This could be quite the score for Interpol."

"Yeah, but it isn't anything we signed up for." I nudged him. "How's about we get back to our party and *then* tip off your Czech cops."

"I will never forgive myself, but I agree with Mercury," Dominic said. "Our mission profile is to counter extradimensional threats, not interdict antiques theft."

"Mission profile?" Brandon shook his head. "Listen to you guys. What good are powers if we're not going to use the blessing we've been given for good no matter where we are? No matter what we face?"

Teget cleared his throat, softly, because, you know, we were still hiding. "I must side with the knight of the skies. Brandon is an honorable man, Mercury, and we would do best to heed his warning."

All I wanted to "heed" was another cup of coffee, preferably one heavy with sugar—and maybe a splash of brandy.

"You're outvoted," Ramos murmured.

"Democracy sucks." I rocked back on my heels, like a surly, well-dressed gargoyle. "Fine. Investigate or whatever. But I'm not sticking around for these guys to notice us."

The gavel struck below. A silver-haired woman of Asian descent claimed her box full of old pottery. She made the credit card transaction in full view of the crowd and claimed a couple of the tattooed mafia as escorts.

"Next lot is, of course, why we are all here," Spikes said. "The item's value is incalculable. The relics we have seen tonight—jewelry, paintings, sculptures—these are all of great historic sentiment. But this is the progenitor of legends. It is more than wealth. It is power."

I had a five-second fantasy in which these rich criminals wheeled out the Ark of the Covenant and were promptly cremated, Nazi style. No such luck. Spiky prompted the crowd into applause as a young, beautiful blonde walked up to the stage from the midst of the crowd.

A woman whose walk I instantly recognized and whose face, when revealed, punched me in the gut.

"*Ay de mí*," Ramos whispered.

Serena Cyr winked at the crowd assembled before her. Her hair was cut short, sleek, not the athletic ponytail I'd seen a few months ago, and her black dress was far more elegant—and form-fitting—than the business casual of a Department of Homeland Security agent. I guess when you go on the run after betraying all of mankind to the insane plans of a tech mogul who's been spliced with the demonic presence calling the shots in the Interstice you're allowed a wardrobe change.

Brandon leaned forward. "Isn't she—?"

"One of the bad guys who was at the fall of Procyon," I said. "The one who partnered with Alexander Arkwright and was responsible for stealing a chunk of Procyon's secrets from the Historic Vaults. What I don't get is what she's doing in Poland at an antiques auction?"

"Maybe she's stealing and selling to finance her life on the run," Ramos said. "She must have connections both sides through her Homeland work."

"Perhaps she merely has an object of great value

with which she wishes to part." Teget's hand shook.

Serena removed a black sword from the next box.

You heard me. *The* black sword. The same one forged in Meda, used by my cousin Crux in his fight against us—until Arkwright betrayed and murdered him right in front of me, using Teget's ax. The black blade's edges glittered in the harsh fluorescent lamps, but the flat sides themselves absorbed all light. Last time I'd seen it, the sword had grown and spawned a counterpart. For the moment, it looked like a fancier, thicker version of a *katana.*

"I do not understand," Teget whispered. "The blade of Crux harnessed the powers of the Interstice. It cannot be wielded in battle by the likes of these Earth lords."

"Something tells me these 'lords' don't care. Either that, or they've got a plan in mind." I glanced at Dominic. "We've got to get that back."

"And whatever else might be here, stolen from Procyon."

I shook my head. "One fight at a time. Teget and I will take the guards by the upper door. Then you can zip-zap down there and yeet the sword out of—"

"Did you just use *yeet* in a sentence?" Brandon groaned. "You sound like my teenaged son."

"No interruptions, Gen X."

"He's not wrong," Ramos said.

I pantomimed zipping my lips shut. "So, Dominic, *portal* down there and *toss* the sword. Brandon? Make sure anybody down there with guns doesn't have a target. You know. Shields."

"Check."

"I can disable weapons much more subtly." Dominic rolled up his cuffs. The Echo Watches sparkled. "It's a simple matter of making them too hot to handle."

"No, I need you to portal."

"What do you expect me to do?" Ramos drew his gun. "Let me lay down covering fire."

"No! No way. None of us are shooting anyone."

"Unless you blast them with the pulsar stave," Dominic pointed out.

"I forgot he could do that," Brandon said thoughtfully.

"Guys!" I hissed. "Talk about herding cats. The plan is the plan! Ramos, you get outside and call for Interpol or whatever passes for the feds in Eastern Europe."

Teget tugged on my sleeve.

"What do you want?"

But it was Serena who spoke up. "The item I've brought you isn't listed on the encrypted emails you received—well, not directly. It's a sword of unparalleled power. Certainly you've at least heard passing rumor of the cataclysmic events surrounding San Camillo, California over the past half year. Let me assure you—they're all true. The worse it sounds, the closer to reality."

Her pause sparked a flurry of murmurs, interspersed with chuckles that sounded, let's say, mildly derisive. More accurate? Some guys down there thought she was nuts.

"Wild tales? They are. But what will convince you more of this is a demonstration—a demonstration of the sword's powers which, when triggered by the right person, can be unleashed." Serena gestured stage right. "Let's bring out our accessories."

A meaty *slap* cracked across the muted conversations. A girl's voice, broke followed by whimpering. Four of the guards led out a ragged line of young women, ranging in age from eighteen to 30, by my guess. They were of varying heights and ethnicities, but the ones who weren't Asian had a few subtle features that their distant bloodline might hail from that part of the world. They were of varying heights and ethnicities, but the ones who weren't Asian had a few subtle features that their distant bloodline might hail from that part of the world.

"You've all done your best to narrow down the right genetic combination. The rest depends on who fits the bill—who is chosen to wield the sword. If it's your offering to the auction, then I'll be glad to pay handsomely for her." Serena turned to the first girl, a brunette with eyes rimmed with runny mascara. She handed the sword hilt-first. "Take it."

The brunette gaped, her eyes wide with fear. My teeth ground as she raised her hands, because her wrists had been rubbed raw by zip ties or rope.

"Guess we can add human trafficking to her list of sins," Ramos murmured.

"She is testing them." Teget's voice shook. "Testing to see who has the bloodlines of Meda that will allow her to use the sword, to capture its powers."

"And whoever the lucky winner is gets sold by one of those mafia guys." I dug an earbud from my pocket and planted it home. Dialed up the playlist on my phone. No way was I gonna take on this fight without tunes. "It's party time."

"Hang on." Brandon pulled a black ski mask over his face and undid his tie.

Ramos and I shared a puzzled look. "Do you seriously travel with one all the time?" I asked.

"Let's just say the last fancy night out on the town I spent ended with an explosion."

Dominic cleared his throat. He handed out ski masks to everyone, though these were dark gray.

Teget and Ramos donned theirs without comment, but I held mine, irritated thoughts rubbing together. No way that was a happy coincidence.

"Yell at me later," Dominic said through his mask. "But let's stop the sword from leaving here."

Another slap. Judging by the blood flowing from between the brunette's fingers as she clutched her nose, she'd failed the test. One of the guards shoved her into the crowd. Serena sighed. "We'll start bidding on her in a minute. Still ought to bring a high price for whatever use you have in mind. On to our next contestant."

Next contestant?

I willed the pulsar stave to life. "Teget? Now."

We hurtled along the catwalk. Light streaked with us. Those guards saw us, sure, but when they turned, guns in hand, it was in slow motion to us. Easy to bat the guns aside—or in my case, melt the firearm as I bashed one guard in the chin. Teget put the ax across the shoulder of the other guard, driving him a foot off the ground and rebounding off the wall.

Subtle? Nope. But that was the plan. Everyone shouted at once. A dozen or more men pulled guns. And every fancy-dressed criminal below had their eyes on us.

Bingo.

There was a flare of light behind us. Dominic appeared, masked, among the imprisoned young women. He reached for the sword.

But the guard nearest him grabbed his shoulder and hurled him ten feet across the stage.

The guard, with Polish mafia tattoos, who had black eyes ringed with glowing purple.

"Oh, great," I muttered. "Syndax."

Then the next young woman in line, one tall and athletic under rumpled T-shirt and jeans, touched the sword. She shuddered, and her expression went from abject terror to soft, sultry joy.

The sword hummed, because she willed it to life.

And gunfire exploded all around us.

CHAPTER FOUR

For about one quarter of a second, I was sure we were all dead. Because when a bunch of people with semi-automatic pistols shoot at you, well, that's a lot of bullets. And I don't like bullets that are sent my way at high velocities.

But that's what we had Airfoil for.

Brandon stood at the railing, arms outstretched, fingers spread. I couldn't see what his medallion did, because its powers—unlike the pulsar stave's blazing energies—were invisible, but when the bullets hit his shield, everybody knew it.

Sparks rippled across the air in a broad stretch that me, Teget, and Ramos were on the other side of. Fourth of July had nothing on the light show. Even better? The shield threw the deflected bullets down to the lower floor, where another row of sparks erupted. Gunmen and the unarmed partygoers scattered, screams carrying for the rafters.

The instant the gunshots shut down, I vaulted

over the railing. Didn't even have to look and see if Teget followed. I knew he had my back, always.

And, you know, his war cry drowned out all other noise.

Dominic staggered upright, clutching his arm. The woman with the sword stood like statue in the middle of swirling chaos. She twisted the blade before her, and I swore I could see a purple tinge spreading to the corners of her eyes. Gone was the cowering figure. Her posture was better than any Marine called to attention.

I landed twenty feet from the stage. "Hand over the sword."

Serena grinned. "The mask is cute. Not as fancy as your usual wardrobe. Not as dashing, either. Sword's right there, Mercury, but no one's taking it away until I get paid for it."

"Are you seriously—Hold on." I popped a guard in the nose with the butt end of the pulsar stave. *Crack* went his nose and *crunch* went his jaw. Look. I didn't feel great about it. It pained me to hurt people like that, because I could imagine what they went through in recovery. The ache in my leg reminded me every second.

But it didn't hurt me as much as it hurt them.

Teget swept the ax across two more attackers, dropping them to the floor. That was impressive enough, but then Brandon flew down from balcony, bringing with him the limp forms of the two guys my brother and I had walloped in our initial attack.

Of course, now other bad guys had Dominic at gunpoint, so I guess it was a draw.

"Right, so …" I waved toward myself. "Gimme the sword."

"You brought your entire entourage? I'm impressed. You've matured some. Not much, but we can't have everything, can we?" Serena gestured to the sword. "This woman can unlock a lot of doors, Mercury. Don't tell me you're not the least bit curious."

I rolled my eyes. "Nope."

I pushed past her for the woman with the sword. She swept it around in a clumsy strike that I deflected, sending a shower of sparks into the air. Not bad for a kidnapped girl who looked like she was on her way to a Goth concert.

But then the ferocity of her strikes increased. So did their speed, and when I parried and went for a swipe of my own, she dodged with a skill that improved every second we were locked in battle.

The bad guys—Syndax Multinational's favorite mercenaries? New recruits? Who cares!—took that as their sign to close in for the kill.

Teget launched into their midst, a madman consumed with lust for battle. He broke arms, slashed through shirts, smashed weapons.

Brandon used the two unconscious men like a snowplow, barreling aside a handful, then landed in their midst. An invisible wave, like a huge wind, sent everyone around him tumbling. "Get out of here while you still can!" he hollered at the noncombatants and aimed for the big doors.

They battered open and people ran, screaming.

Meanwhile, I was getting tired of the dueling. I backed up into a defensive stand, and sword lady did the same.

Then I whipped the pulsar stave's end over and blasted her with a burst of concentrated tachyons.

She smashed through the plywood walls at the back of the stage.

Which had the added benefit of giving a Dominic a chance to aim an Echo Watch at the gun of the guy holding him hostage. The weapon glowed impossibly bright, like I was staring straight into a flashlight, and the guard yelled. He dropped his gun. Smoke rose from blackened fingertips.

Dominic struck him in the face until he toppled.

I launched myself over his head, riding high on the energies of the pulsar stave that infused not just the suit, but my prosthetic leg and every cell of my body. I aimed for the hole in the wall the woman had created, figuring out how I was gonna land without killing her.

Turned out, didn't have to, because she was already leaping toward me.

We collided in a *whump* of flesh and bone, accompanied by a flash of pent-up power. Our tangle of limps crashed onto the stage, making a two-person dent. Pretty sure there was another dent in my spine.

And the whole time, Serena stood there, arms

folded, smirk curving her lips. Man. I can't believe I kind of had the hots for her.

Don't tell Loredana.

"Freeze!"

Ramos? I told him to get lost and get Interpol! Instead, he had his pistol in a two-handed grip, aiming for Serena's chest. Because *of course* he did.

"This is great." She chuckled. "Am I under arrest? We're well outside city limits—by a few thousand miles."

"Hey," I croaked. "That's my line."

"You'll hand over the sword or I will shoot you." Ramos' stance never wavered.

"You will? You'll shoot an unarmed woman in a foreign country? A federal agent?"

"Pretty sure Homeland fired you." I let Dominic help me up. Where was sword lady?

She'd walked off like she was on her way to powder her nose, but instead of going to the restroom, she wound up at the box where Serena had set the Greek pottery.

Brandon stepped in front of her. "Stay put. I'll take that sword."

The woman stabbed so fast I was surprised Brandon had a chance to erect his shields. Even more surprised when the blade sparked, slowed, and then continued through. It cut his jacket and left a red stain on his ribcage.

He winced and fell onto his knees.

The woman turned and faced Serena.

"Do it," she said.

The woman brought the sword crashing down.

"No!" Ramos spun and fired.

Serena kicked, sweeping his legs out from underneath. The shot buried itself in the ceiling. Next thing I knew, she was astride Ramos' chest, the pistol in her hands, the muzzle buried under his chin.

I was too dazed to react. I was sure I was gonna hear the sickening slash of metal through flesh. But instead, pottery shattered.

The woman had broken the pot worth tens of thousands of dollars. Shards littered the floor.

"Release me!" Teget? He had eight guys holding him down, eight men with eyes turned black and tinged purple. Great I hadn't realized how many of her hoodlums Serena had juiced up on the tachyon-infused serum Arkwright had developed for his Syndax soldiers, the stuff that could make them almost equal to me or Teget or another Medan warrior in strength.

"Okay, let's not get crazy." I held the pulsar staves ready, watching both the sword woman and the henchmen surrounding Teget. "Bet we can figure this out."

"You are ones who attacked us." That was Spikes.

"Nobody asked you." I gestured to Serena. "Let our gang go and we'll leave with the sword."

"Too late for that," Serena said. "She's already proven more valuable than I'd hoped—and there's no way I'm separating her from that blade. Make sure to tell Ms. Lark and the rest of the people at Procyon I'm grateful they shared their files. Otherwise, I never would have found Xia."

A hissing built, like sand being poured down a tube. It intensified, and I thought one of the air vents overhead was gonna bust open, until Xia—Serena pronounced it "Shia," in one syllable—waved her sword through a writhing tendril of glittering grains. Kind of like sand, to fit with the sound effects, but with maroonish, ruddy streaks.

It swirled around the sword, and when Xia slashed the air, the grains shotgunned in all directions.

The first spray struck Brandon's mask. He arched his back, gagging, as the particles soaked through the fabric, poured up his nose, and filtered into his eyes.

Another tendril enveloped Teget, muffling his cries. His guards had to drop back before the spray infiltrated them.

Still another edge of the spray hit Ramos at the same moment. Serena backed away, but the sand or particles of whatever we were dealing with didn't seem interested in her.

"Ramos?" I took a step toward him.

"Don't ..." His voice broke into a discordant array of sounds, with human words drowned under what I heard as screeching electronics.

The particles banked sharply, like Airfoil in pursuit of a bad guy, and came straight for my face.

"Mercury!"

A hand hit my shoulder and light blasted my

vision—light, then dark, accompanied by the worst stomach drop since I'd done five roller coaster rides back to back.

Dominic's loft materialized around me, hazy, warm, and indistinct.

I braced myself on the wood floor for just a second, and then the portal flared to life again.

We reappeared on the balcony. It took about five seconds, maybe less, and if I blinked, I thought I could see an afterimage of where I'd been. I swayed toward the railing.

"Easy," Dominic said. "When I travel that fast, the side effects can be disorienting."

"No kidding." I grabbed onto the railing and focused on making sure the room quit spinning.

There weren't many people left in said room. Serena's squad of enforcers were all on their way out, exiting behind the plywood walls at the back of the stage. The other doors leading back into Klub Rozsada were flung wide open. No missing the shouts, or the general noise of mayhem, because the music had stopped.

And the weird keening of European sirens leaked in.

"We'd better get moving," Dominic said.

"Not without the rest of our people." Problem was, none of our people were in a hurry to leave. They stood stock-still, slouched over, facing each other in a ragged triangle.

I leapt over the railing and landed—in a heap,

because my prosthetic leg buckled underneath. I almost wound up flopped on my side.

Didn't seem to bother Xia as she used the sword to—what was she doing with it? Playing around like it was a vacuum, siphoning up the particles into neat, sharp ridges on the blade.

"Like I said, I owe Procyon a lot." Serena put her hands on Xia's shoulder. "Like revealing to me the legend of symmachites. Old Greek tales, tracked all the way up through the Second World War. Legends that told of their unpredictability, which made them useless, until Alexander whispered to me the secrets of the dark blade. Your idiot cousin didn't understand its subtlety."

"Kinda hard for him get subtle when your boyfriend betrayed and murdered him," I snapped. "Immobilizing these guys isn't gonna stop me from wiping you two across the floor."

"Sure it is." Serena whispered in Xia's ear. Xia nodded, without breaking her midnight gaze with me. The purple light ringing her irises intensified. "Because we don't need to do anything."

Xia brought the blade's tip to her nose and inhaled a flurry of the symmachites. She murmured, so quietly, I couldn't hear anything but the *shush* of her breath.

But Ramos, Teget, and Brandon heard more than a wordless nothing. They leapt at us, in unison.

There was no finesse to their attack. Teget swung wildly with the ax, his blows jagged. I'd never seen him fight like that. I blocked with the stave, blows raining between us. "Hey! Teget! Snap out of this! She's got you!"

He wasn't even looking at me. A swirling, maroon haze covered his eyes as he continued a brutal attack. I could drop him—a quick Taser-like burst to the back of the neck—but I was more worried about Brandon, who was hurtling toward Dominic.

You know, Airfoil, the guy who could crush things with gravity.

Dominic blinked out, then reappeared back to back with me. The Echo Watches whined as he fired on Brandon, their blasts sizzling the air.

Ramos fired at me.

I dropped to the ground. Bullets whipped overhead. I split the stave into halves and sped into Ramos with the daintiness of a charging bull on crack.

The collision smacked him against a wall. He dropped his gun.

"Ramos," I panted. "Buddy?"

He glared past me, eyes the same vacant and stormy ones as Teget's.

A sudden blow smashed me to the floor. Dominic cried out.

Yeah, that would be Brandon's gravity powers.

We squirmed under the invisible force pressing us into the concrete. It was getting harder to breathe.

"I hate it when things turn out this easy." Serena and Xia approached. Serena knelt by me, three feet away. She must have been just outside Brandon's field. "Xia will make your death quick. Like a guillotine."

"I bet she will," I gasped, "But I've had enough for one evening."

The stave's energies flared. Brandon's field? It fizzled out.

See, I'd already tangled with him as Airfoil when we were on… Less friendly terms. And figured out a tachyon-enhanced relic like mine could pierce his powers. Same as Xia had managed with the sword.

Except the stave was far stronger.

I threw one at Brandon's head. He froze it in midair, but I was already leaping up, the second one unleashing at blast at his chest—right where he hung that stupid medallion. There was a flash, and a shout from him, before we tumbled back down. I snagged the half of the stave I'd thrown.

Dominic caught me. I could feel the rising breeze from the Echo Watches' portal. "Come on!"

"No! Not without—!"

I was stepping away, reaching for Teget, when the portal blew outwards. Our cluster vanished.

And I was back in Dominic's loft.

Except, so was everybody else.

For a split second, Ramos, Teget, and Brandon stared at me, as Serena and Xia materialized right next to us.

"Well, crap," I croaked.

Brandon raised his hands and I knew we were royal toast, so I did the only thing I could think of—I channeled every last spare bit of energy back into the pulsar stave and delivered a shockwave that threw everyone against the walls.

Even Dominic.

Then I lunged at him, grabbed his wrists, and hollered, "Go!"

Still glassy-eyed, he got the Echo Watches spinning …

Face first into snow.

The air was cold, bitter, and damp. And me wearing nice party clothes and a ruined suit jacket. The shivering took over as soon as the adrenaline dropped off.

Dominic's teeth chattered. He was sitting on his butt, ankles in snow, down in this—drainage ditch? "G-good p-plan."

I collapsed onto the frozen banks. "W-Worst bachelor party ever."

CHAPTER FIVE

Not Gdansk, not Paris, and definitely not San Camillo.

Dominic had beamed us to Drake City. In New England. In December. *Outside.*

Good news was, we were in the same place he'd landed us when we came here in the fall, trying to establish first contact with Airfoil for our showdown against Arkwright and his evil, sentient relic, the Hedron of Orbits. And being Christmas break, the grounds of Gunnison State College were deserted.

So there weren't any witnesses as we trudged through the four inches of snow covering the walking path winding around the edge of campus.

"We'd better make contact with Procyon." Dominic spoke through clenched teeth, I assumed because if he tried normal talking, the chattering from the cold would knock out so many chompers he'd need dentures. "They need to know what's happened."

"Yeah, I get that. Wasn't planning to dial 9-1-1." I used my fingers as an imaginary phone. "Hello, Emergency? Your local superhero's been brainwashed by a villain—oh, and so has a warrior from another dimension and a California city cop. Sure, I'll hold."

"Will you stop it?" Dominic snapped. "This is serious."

"No kidding." I willed the pulsar stave to life and separated its halves. One went into the custom holster under my shirt. Warmth trickled between my ribs. "Here, want one?"

"That's not a toy."

"You're right, it's a powerful weapon capable of dismembering monsters. It's also a source of heat when used properly." *Like on lukewarm slices of pizza.* Probably best if I didn't share that thought. "We're stuck together. Let's not freeze to death before we hit the first marker, okay?"

Dominic glared at me, but he took the half of the pulsar stave and stuck it in his waistband, between his shirts. "Thanks."

"No problem."

We trudged on, our classy dress shoes poor snow boots. Their crunching through the icy top layer was the only sound nearby. Drake City's roar of traffic, broken by the occasional siren, surrounded campus.

"*The Empire Strikes Back*?" Dominic asked.

"What?"

"Reaching the first marker. That's from *Empire*. Those space horses—"

"Tauntauns. Two-legged."

"Oh. I thought they rode horses—"

I held up a hand. "Look, I appreciate the attempt, but please don't mess up the reference."

"Right." Dominic made a face. "Why haven't you called Procyon yet?"

"Me? I thought the *we* in 'We need to call Procyon' meant *you*."

"I…" Dominic sighed.

"What, are you out of battery?"

"No. We do need to talk about it, though."

"About… your phone? Look, I'm not in the mood for word games."

Dominic pulled his phone from his pocket. Typical smartphone, except for the module attached to the back. It was a slender, black oval with a white triple outline. Gold lights flickered in a triple curve along one side.

"Tachyon dowser," Dominic said. "Liz designed it a few months ago, during the ongoing inventory of items lost after the destruction of Procyon headquarters revealed that Crux's sword was missing."

"A tachyon dowser. Like, for tracking down relics that emit a tachyon signature. For tracking the sword." A pounding sensation grew in my head, right behind my eyeballs. It matched my heart's acceleration. "Handy thing to have on a bachelor party night, isn't it?"

"Intelligence put down a few possible sightings."

"Serena sightings."

"Yes."

"Lemme guess—Paris and Gdansk."

"Those were the first two on my list."

I glowered at the asphalt patches in the snow. We were at a sidewalk on the edge of the campus. Only question was, where to next? "Did the guys know about this?"

"About …"

"About my bachelor party being a front for a secret mission to nab Serena and the sword that I wasn't told about!" A couple of pigeons sprang off the sidewalk. I wanted to whip out the pulsar stave and blast them.

"They didn't. I hate to use the phrase, but it was a need-to-know kind of operation."

"As in, Operations. Loredana's branch of Procyon. Speaking of …"

"No. This was Alvarez's play. Loredana's just as unaware as you."

"Okay. Good."

Dominic cleared his throat. "Sorry."

"Don't worry about it."

"It's just that, given your relation to Crux … He was family, after all, even if he was estranged. Alvarez felt that connection was too close to risk the operation."

"I said, don't worry about it. Which is Mercury-speak for, 'Please shut up.' We'll worry about not telling each other things later." I closed my eyes. This was a bad dream, right? I was gonna wake up on my couch—or even in a chair in a Parisian restaurant. I peeked. No such luck.

"At least you know why I had a pocket full of ski masks," Dominic said brightly.

"Yeah. Good planning on your part. But Brandon—"

"I really think he carries one at all times."

"Right." I shivered. Pulsar stave or no pulsar stave, the wind off Sculpin Bay was knifing right through my bones. "We need to get indoors and get a change of clothes. And something to eat."

"We've already had lunch and dinner."

I checked my watch. Late afternoon? Jet lag slammed into me, and my tiredness exploded into full-blown exhaustion. Daytime then late night then daytime again … My head swam. "First thing's first."

I dialed home.

Two rings and Liz was right on it. Her sigh was so long I thought she'd deflate. "Mercury? Again? It's only been a few hours. There's really nothing—"

"Can it. Dom—Gemini and I are stranded in Drake City. We ran into Serena Cyr in Paris and she found a person with Medan genetic code to activate Crux's sword so they could wrangle ancient evil nanites and then brainwashed Brandon, Teget, and Ramos into fighting us."

"I—oh. Oh. That'd bad."

"Yeah, you think? Extraction would be nice."

"I better call Ms. Lark first. And Manager Alvarez—"

"Whoa, whoa, Alvarez?" No way I wanted to deal with that condescending paper-pusher after this mess. He'd probably ask me to sign a couple of forms before I concocted a new plan. "Forget about him. Get me a plane. Our allies-turned-bad guys are stuck in Dominic's apartment."

"At the entrance to the Transect?"

I stared at the phone a moment, lost for a reply.

"Gateway and tunnel from this Earth to an alternate one," Dominic said. "Home to my doppelganger."

"The evil doppelganger?"

"Yes."

"Super." I shook my head. "Liz, you get all that?"

"Okay, um, yes, but they shouldn't be able to gain access to that portal. Except Teget has the ax, right? He could activate the Transect like he's done before to travel to the Interstice. Maybe ..."

"Fine. So, get ahold of Procyon in Rampart. Have them send their security over to, uh, secure the apartment."

"On it." Her fingers clattered on a keyboard. "What else do you need?"

"Snow pants," Dominic murmured.

"Friendly contacts here."

"One sec ..." Liz hummed. "Messaging you a number. Tyrone Thomas, Operations supervisor of the Drake City office."

"Thanks."

"What about Ms. Lark? Did you guys call her?"

"No, don't worry about it. I don't think she was in on this operation." I glared at Dominic.

"Oh. Okay. I'll contact Procyon in Rampart and see what they've picked up with their sensing equipment. Maybe they can give us some hints about what Serena's up to."

"What're the odds Alvarez won't find out?"

"If I ask the right people, we should be okay. Alvarez is still new and, um, sometimes he's not very nice."

"There's an understatement. No, don't worry about that part. We'll take care of it. Thanks, Liz."

"See ya!"

I ended the call and handed Dominic back his phone. "Here. You call the Drake City office. Tell this Tyrone guy he'd better be the one to contact the Rampart people and have them send in security,"

"Sure." Dominic punched up the number Liz provided. "Anything else?"

"Yeah, but you're not going to like it."

"If there wasn't something I objected to, Mercury, I'd wonder about you."

Guess he was getting to know me better. "Brandon's son. The little punk who hung up on me when we were fighting that fiery fiend this fall? He knows about Airfoil. Called himself a partner when I labeled him a sidekick."

"I'm sorry, are you wanting us to reach out to a teenager for support?" Dominic frowned. Fortunately, his lips weren't turning blue.

"We don't have a lot of choice in the matter. This isn't like finding out an astral fiend's gonna come charging out of a rip. We've seen Airfoil in action in a big way—he held up the entire San Camillo Bay in midair, for crying out loud! You think Procyon can handle him? I'm not sure the Air Force could."

"But someone close might be able to get through to him, if we can pierce his powers."

"Bingo. We already know the stave and your Echo Watches can do the trick. Of course, he'll be harder to distract with Ramos and Teget …" I lost the rest of the sentence, and the idea that created it, as I pictured my brother and the guy who was closer to me than any dad I'd ever had.

"I'm sure they're okay," Dominic said.

"Yeah. I know. I'm not looking forward to fighting them. Teget's a warrior; he can handle a beating. But Ramos is a regular guy, even with his training and whatever the symmachite creatures have done to him. This kid, dumb as it seems, could give us a psychological advantage." I indicated our surroundings. "At this point, I'll take all the help we can get."

Dominic nodded and placed the call to Procyon's Drake City office. I texted the number Brandon had provided. <Sean, it's Mercury Hale. Your dad's in trouble. The bad guys have him under their control. We escaped but need help beyond the usual. And a place to warm up.>

We kept walking. No way I was gonna have

Dominic fire up his portals again, because we'd have to zap back to his loft.

And I didn't want to face who or what could be waiting. Not yet.

The address came through, without any personal greetings. "Nine Square."

"It's a neighborhood not far from here, northeast. Quiet. Between Hull district and Gunnison."

"Super. More Millennials and college kids."

Dominic sighed. "You could easily fit both categories."

"So could you."

"Of the two of us, who has a steady, normal job, a wife, a house, and a nice car?"

"Don't forget the dog."

"What about Sammy?"

I plucked a blond hair from his shirt. "Unless your wife's taken to dyeing her black locks, Sammy's a Golden Retriever. Also, I have a steady job. Probably pays better than yours."

"I did say *normal*."

"Okay, *Gemini*, the portal-producer who's been tracking down evil doppelgangers from an alternate Earth."

"I mean the architectural consulting I do for Procyon—"

"Fine, yes. You're stable, I'm not." I tapped my chest. "But I'm in charge."

Dominic chuckled. "That's great. Not all your

jokes are funny, you know."

I just shook my head. We made the rest of the walk in a gloomy silence, which got more sullen every block. It wasn't until I rang the buzzer to the tidy brick apartment complex on Twelfth Street that Dominic piped up with, "I have seniority."

"Really."

"Of course. My position as an operative—"

"Is at least a year behind mine, maybe two. And if you're gonna argue that you have a direct line to Loredana, I got news: Mine's *way* more direct."

"That's crass."

"I didn't mean … Not like that."

"*Geez, you two.*" The voice crackling out of the speaker by the front door sounded as exasperated as the two of us put together. "*You're as bad as the old guys whining about their property taxes after church.*"

"Sean? It's Mercury."

"*Duh. I can read text messages. Unlike old people.*"

"Uh, okay. I was serious. There's—" We were out in the open. A guy walked his dog by, earbuds in place, scrolling through images. The terrier yipped at Dominic. "There's a problem with your dad. As in, he's not himself."

The speaker went staticky. A sigh? A pensive silence? Maybe muffled profanity? My guess was some combo of the three. "*Dad said he was going out to a party with you guys. Bachelor stuff.*"

"Turns out there was a secret mission behind it. Not everybody was telling the truth."

"There's a shocker. Okay."

For a minute I thought he'd blown us off but then the door unlocked.

"See? Piece of cake?" I grinned at Dominic.

He pushed past me and headed upstairs.

Sean met us at the apartment door. Tall, skinny, like all teenaged boys are at one point. A lot of resemblance to his dad in and around the eyes, right down to the freckles, but the air was brown, an unruly mop. He chewed on his lip. "Hey."

"Hey, kid. Mercury Hale." I offered a hand.

"Borrow some of Dad's clothes." He turned away and started typing on his phone. "Then we gotta go. I'm calling an Uber."

"Go? We just got here. And we're supposed to meet with some … allies here in the city."

"Then tell them to wait or something. I told Frank we'd be at his place in like fifteen minutes once he gave me directions."

"Frank. A friend of your dad's?"

"Sort of. Like a cranky uncle. But he trained dad."

"Look, no offense, but last thing we need right now is the Obi-wan type."

"Yeah?" Sean held up his phone. It played a YouTube video from a few months ago. I recognized the date. It was around the time Airfoil had single-handedly stopped a gang of terrorists lead by the local supervillain from turning Drake City into his personal kingdom.

But Sean showed us an armored scout car blasting apart a convoy of SUVs.

"Frank," he said.

"Okay." I nodded. "Lead the way."

CHAPTER SIX

The Uber driver was a bald white guy with glasses so thick they could have been made of bulletproof glass. He didn't speak. I mean, not a single word. Didn't make eye contact, either.

Just as well. I wasn't in a chatty mood.

I know, right? That's how you know things were bad.

My breath fogged the window of a Ford Taurus that looked like it hadn't been out of a garage since it had been featured as a "futuristic" car in *Robocop*. Same lousy gray color, too.

"Yes, sir. I understand." Dominic had his phone pressed to his ear. "6 o'clock. We'll be there."

I waited until he ended the call. "Procyon?"

"Tyrone Thomas. We're to meet with him this evening."

Argh. This evening. Part of my body thought it was still late night. Another part told me I'd eaten lunch and dinner and there was no way I should be hungry. And tired. "He have a plan in mind? Besides us beaming back to Rampart and hoping we don't get whipped?"

"He's been in touch with Rampart office. They sent security over to my loft."

"And? You should have led with that."

"Empty." Dominic leaned against the upholstered headrest. I wanted to tell him he'd better show if he was gonna do that. "They're searching the city."

"I wouldn't bother. They're either trying to track us down, or they've gone back to Meda for the night's blade." The though chilled me worse than the gray winter weather outside. "If Teget uses the ax combined with it, the bad guys will be one step closer to permanently open a path between our Earth and the Interstice."

"Which you've already avoided. The Battle of North Beach."

"Finally, somebody gets it right." I shifted in my seat. Brandon's shirt was a size too large for me. Who knew a librarian was so built? Guy must do pushups in his sleep—or with a book drop on his spine. Dominic and I were both wearing items from his wardrobe.

"You guys wanna shut up for like five seconds?" Sean was punching away at his phone.

"How many texts have you sent your dad?"

"A lot." He glared at us. "He's not answering."

"I don't think brainwashed super—" Dominic elbowed me, then pointed at our mute driver. Right.

Operational secrecy. "Parents are big on returning messages, kid."

"He's never ignored them. Except if he told me ahead of time he was going off-channel."

"He's left you with no way to contact him?"

"Just a couple times." Sean frowned at the phone screen. "He went on these missions for a few days … Never said where he went or what he was doing. But he's been weird since he fought Domitian. No, wait … Since the party after that. Something spooked him."

"If he's leaving you out of it, there's probably a good reason for staying tight-lipped," Dominic offered.

"Yeah, whatever." Sean tapped the driver's shoulder. "Up here, on the right."

We were on the state highway winding up the coast away from Newport, Drake City's grimy industrial suburb. The sprawling train yards were a mile behind. Pine trees hemmed the road in on both sides, allowing only fleeting glimpses of the slate-colored Atlantic Ocean between clustered trunks to our right. Not much out there except scattered driveways.

The car pulled over onto a dirt shoulder. A short, gravel path disappeared into the trees. No address marker. No mailbox. Not even a power line.

Dominic passed the driver a few bucks for a tip. "Thank you."

I watched the guy drive off as I zipped up a Hull Branch Library sweatshirt against the cold. "You're, ah, not gonna make him wait?"

Sean snickered. "Dude. Do you even know how Uber works?"

"Listen, kid." I pointed a finger at him.

"Yeah?" Sean watched me like a cat contemplating if it wanted one mouse or two for lunch.

"You're grounded." I brushed past him on the way up the gravel driveway.

I heard a grumble that sounded like, "Not my parent," but let it pass.

We rounded the bend of pines into a clearing home to two buildings—a shed with a brown metal roof and corrugated steel sides, and the house. Which, it should be noted, was made out of a shipping container. Scratch that: Two of them, welded side by side, set on sturdy posts. The end farthest perched on two huge metal and concrete supports set into the rocky coastline, where the Atlantic's waves churned against black boulders. The nearest end featured a wooden porch, home to a forlorn flowerpot and a sagging Adirondack chair. Smoke hung in a haze over the clearing, a gift from the narrow aluminum chimney.

"That's impressive." Dominic craned his neck as we approached porch. "The roof's cantilevered. Looks like the builder incorporated an attic into the space between. Choosing wood paneling for the exterior accents was risky, though, given the climate."

I rolled my eyes. "Let's get the number of his architect so you bros can compare notes."

"Well, I would be interested to know how he—"

"Kidding!" I grabbed his shoulder and aimed him for the porch. "Ring the bell."

Dominic frowned. "I think the homeowner's aware of our arrival."

Okay, so I'd missed the security camera in its tiny black dome over the door. And missed that the door wasn't a lovely entrance welcoming visitors. Nope. Solid steel, with a tiny slot for a window. Come to think of it, most of the windows on the home's flank were small portholes, except for the long glimmers of glass at the far end.

"No sweat." I rapped my knuckles on cold, wet metal. No sign of a doorknob.

The door swung in. I caught a glimpse of flannel and blue jeans. And a gun.

Of course it was a weapon. Because apparently nobody greeted me at a door with a smile and a handshake. I missed Jack Jackson.

The guy had a shotgun pointed at my stomach. A shotgun with a magazine attached that was as long as its barrel.

"No soliciting." He chambered a shell. Didn't need to. The voice itself would have stopped me in my tracks. It made me happy I wasn't a selling carpet cleaner.

"Um, you know, signs are cheaper." I kept my hands at my sides.

"Still." The guy was stone-faced, with a salt-pepper mix of dark and silver hair. The beard gave him the craggy features of George Clooney. You know, less *The Peacemaker* and more an updated version of *Syriana*. But less charming,

Sean pushed between me and Dominic. "Quit it, Frank. They're like dad's superfriends."

"Great. I feel much better about them turning up on my doorstep." Frank aimed the shotgun at the porch. "Superheroes. What a joke. I don't see any leotards, though, so that makes you somewhat smarter than Brandon."

"As fun as it is standing out in the cold and getting insulted by a stranger, how's about you let us in so we can deal with our pressing problem?" I snapped. "Namely, your protégé getting brainwashed."

"Sean told me."

"Seems like you're doing a lousy job mentoring if he falls off your radar like that."

"I've been out of the picture for a while. Had to get out of town, as they say." Frank smirked. "Brainwashed, is he? Chalk that up as another reason Brandon never should have gone public. The Garrison keeps its possession of the medallions secret for this exact reason. Those relics are too powerful to lose."

"One hundred percent agree." I gestured at Sean, who tossed his bag on a couch. Inside. Where it wasn't freezing.

"No need to hurry. I've got to vet you boys before—"

Light flashed to my right. Dominic had blinked out. Again.

Frank's shotgun whipped up. "What happened? Where'd he go?"

The return portal opened behind Frank, to his left. Dominic's Echo Watches pulsed, their components still spinning. Frank's shotgun glowed like a toaster's hot coils.

Frank shouted and dropped the gun. Dominic caught it.

I folded my arms and grinned. "How's that for superfriends?"

"Not bad." Frank nodded.

"Sorry about that," Dominic said. "I don't think I damaged the gun too—"

Frank grabbed Dominic's right shoulder and punched him in the stomach. Dominic doubled over, coughing and groaning. Frank retrieved the shotgun and perched the muzzle six inches from my frozen nose. "Not too bad, but sloppy. Come on in. Coffee?"

The house had an open, airy feel for a place build out of a couple shipping containers slapped together. Frank had a fireplace going in the living room, which took the far quarter of his home. Floor to ceiling windows of thick, steel-framed glass treated us to a view of the surging slate waters of the Atlantic beyond the mouth of Sculpin Bay.

"All right, Brandon's brainwashed." Frank offered me a steaming mug. "How so?"

"Thanks." Yow. Hot stuff. As in, blistering

temperature. I slugged back a mouthful anyway. "Brainwashed, as in, ancient nanites. We think."

"Not a reassuring tactical analysis."

I shrugged. "We tend to wing it."

"We being Procyon Foundation?"

I glanced at Dominic, who was holding his mug against his stomach. Still sore, no doubt, from where Frank socked him.

"Time for full disclosure, if you want my help." Frank sipped his coffee, never breaking his stare.

"Procyon Foundation is a charitable organization," Dominic said. "Its primary goal is to better the communities it serves."

"You do a lot of 'bettering' when you kill monsters?" Frank smirked. "I'll put my cards down first, all right? The Garrison is aware of Procyon's true activities, just like I'm sure they have a file on ours."

Dominic cleared this throat. "Well, I—"

I lit up the pulsar stave. Dominic shut up. Frank's hand slipped to the belt line of his jeans, under the edge of his flannel shirt. Concealed carry, much? "This is getting nowhere. Yes, Procyon pays me to kill monsters. You probably heard about the messes we've had out West lately. All true. Okay? So, let's make with the plan to get our friends un-brainwashed."

"That's the best thing a grown-up's said so far today," Sean muttered.

"You knew the deal," Frank said. "You came to me for help? I'm going to assess the situation."

"Oh, come on, Frank. Dad's in trouble! I don't care what your stupid Garrison rules say about getting involved. Let's go meet with their people and see how we can put our forces together."

"Our forces."

"Yeah. Forces." Sean jabbed a finger in Dominic's direction. "He told Mercury about 'security' at Procyon checking something out. And I've seen the videos from San Camillo. There's like dozens of guys in black with automatic weapons! No way they were all cops."

Frank smirked behind his mug. "Procyon has a private army. There's a shocker."

"Well, your sarcasm game is on-point, if nothing else," I said. "But the kid's right. We need every helping hand we can get. I, for one, would rather go up against my brother and a cop and a superhero without Procyon's guys because I want to keep casualties low."

"Smart." Frank drained the last of his coffee. "Bad news for us, of course, but that's the way it goes. Okay. I'll go with you."

"Really? Yes!" Sean pumped his fists.

"That's great. Yeah." I scratched the back of my neck. "Armored vehicle aside—which, by the way, I heard was destroyed—what's your skillset?"

Frank crossed to a handsome cabinet crafted from walnut. He pressed his thumb to a black box affixed to the handles. The cabinet was filled with guns, a dozen and a half that I could see.

"Classically trained, as your generation would say." He drew out a rifle I recognized—SCAR-H, same kind that I'd seen in Procyon's arsenal. "That, and I have some experience with the medallion that Brandon carries. Not that particular one, but close enough."

"Oh, yeah? They let you polish them?"

Frank slammed home a magazine and checked the sights on the rifle. "Only when I wasn't using one for twenty years as a member of the Garrison."

Sean snickered. My cheeks burned. Pretty sure they were the same color as the laser indicator gleaming under the barrel.

Dominic clapped my shoulder. "Very smooth. I think, Mr. Belasco, we'll get along just fine. Let me call us a ride—"

"No. Absolutely not. I'm driving." Frank pulled on a worn leather jacket and slung the rifle on a strap over his shoulder.

Great. Boomer mobile?

Sort of. But not one I was gonna complain about.

That tarp in the shed? It covered up a hardtop Chevy Chevelle, four-door, dark blue with white stripes. When Frank turned the engine over, man, I could have heard it back in Paris.

I couldn't help grinning as we rumbled back into the city, on warm leather seats.

Maybe this bachelor party thing wouldn't turn out so bad.

⌗ ⌗ ⌗

Tyrone Thomas, Operations supervisor of Procyon Foundation's Drake City office, was going to hit his head on the ceiling. No joke.

He was a tall black guy, probably six and a half feet tall, dressed as classy as a guy in Loredana's role should be—in a masculine fashion, of course. Navy-blue suit, white shirt, brown wingtips. His beard and hair are trimmed so well, he and Ramos could have had a grooming contest.

Thinking about Ramos was a bad idea. I slumped into one of the chairs surrounding a table of glass and steel in the curved conference room on the seventh floor.

"I had Tracking put a satellite into play for traces of tachyon emissions." Thomas used his phone to trigger a screen on the far wall. A map of the United States glowed, with Procyon offices marked by white and black diamonds. A red indicator moved steadily away from Rampart. "But we were a bit late getting a move on. Security determined that Airfoil and his accomplices left Rampart on a private jet."

"Hey!" Sean snapped. "My dad's nobody's accomplice."

Frank stood behind Sean, arms crossed. He kicked Sean's chair and put his finger to his lips, shushing the kid.

"Mr. Tusk is flying sans aircraft." Thomas' voice was soothing, which was a bad thing for me because the combination of leftover pizza and rich Thai food—plus a fair amount of alcohol—was not offset by the two cups of coffee I'd consumed. "Tracking got a fix, but it wasn't until the Salt Lake City office phoned screaming that we knew what the situation was."

"I wasn't aware Procyon had an office in Salt Lake," Dominic said.

"Not officially. It's under a holding company." Thomas tapped his phone. The map slid over, replaced by images of a—well, an office. Glass and beige concrete, same as most buildings on its block.

You could tell the Procyon one by the giant hole bashed through the front door.

"Brandon did that?" Frank's voice didn't betray emotion. He could have been commenting on the chance of snow. Still made me squirm.

"Witnesses are unsure of what happened. I've got some slowed-down surveillance footage of a black and white blur. Looks more like a business suit than a suit of armor."

"That would be him." My guts twisted. The sensation had nothing to do with too much or too little food. "Did anyone get hurt?"

"No. Staff issued an evac as soon as the first tremors started."

"Thank God," Dominic murmured.

"So, he took out one of your smaller and more secretive offices," I said. "Unmarked. Right? What about the rest of the gang?"

"The jet's continuing west. We lost track of to where, precisely." Thomas returned us to the map.

"Intelligence got back to us on its registration—fake, like our Salt Lake City office's identity. They peeled back five layers of dummy corporations and pulled up Syndax Multinational."

Dominic winced. I shook my head.

"That's—bad?" Sean frowned.

"You see those videos of crazed 'terrorists,' as the news called them, fighting alongside monsters in San Camillo?"

"Yeah. The ones who might be zombies or be *with* zombies …" Sean's eyes widened. "Oh."

"Oh is right."

"We still don't know how it is Brandon and the others are being controlled," Frank said.

"Hold up. Serena Cyr mentioned symmachites. Ancient Greek, maybe," I pointed out.

Thomas stroked his beard. "That's troublesome and worrying. I heard mention of symmachites in the old Historic Vault files. Semi-smart microscopic machines that could subsume a man's will, make it subject to another's."

"Mind-controlling nanites?" I shook my head. "Let me guess. Medan tech?"

"No one's got a clue where they come from. Not Meda, as best we know."

Even though it meant the mini robots controlling my friends hadn't come from a dimension I knew was stocked with powerful weapons, my unease stuck around.

"Where is the jet headed?" Dominic asked.

"San Camillo. But there's one other hidden office between there and Salt Lake. A listening post, really. Winnemucca, Nevada."

I blinked at the map as he zoomed in the image. "There's—literally nothing out there."

"Sure. Nothing but one of our most sensitive large-scale tachyon arrays. One that relays a boatload of data to the rest of our offices in the U.S." Thomas scowled. "No big deal."

"You're short on time," Frank said. "Airfoil's speed's reaching beyond three hundred miles per hour these days."

"As we estimated." Thomas glanced at me. "If you boys can intercept him at Winnemucca, buy us some time, we can stop him."

Dominic and I looked at each other. "It is the two of us versus him," he said. "We've put up a good fight before."

"That's why we asked," Thomas said. "Our intel indicates you three had a tussle here a few months back."

"Sharp intel." I rubbed my face. "You said you can stop him. What, you have an extra medallion around? Because from what I've heard, only another member of the less-than-awesome Garrison or their evil equivalent can stop somebody with one of those toys."

Thomas glowered at Frank. "Not for lack of trying to reach them."

Frank shrugged.

"No, Mr. Hale, what we have is a decades-old prototype of a weapon—a portable emitter designed to penetrate and disable the powers provided by tachyon-enhanced weaponry such as the pulsar stave. I'm rushing the tech gang through what they'd rather have be methodical research. In a couple hours, we can have a semi-working model."

"Way after Airfoil reaches Winnemucca."

Thomas nodded.

I stood and stretched. "Well, your gang better move fast. Because if we get ourselves stomped, San Camillo's gonna need someone else to point and shoot. Come on, Dominic. Time to beam back to your place."

"This is a hasty idea, but I suppose it's our only option." Dominic rolled up his sleeves.

"The only one in the timeframe." Frank braced himself on the desk. "Tyrone, if your techies get me that gun, I've got a way to deliver it."

"It's not man-portable anymore. We had to mount it because it's producing considerable kickback."

"I've got a set of four wheels perfect for it."

"Better re-think that, Frank." I stood near to Dominic and readied for the vomit-inducing transit through the portal. "Because we can only get it to San Camillo via Dominic's loft in Rampart. So, no tanks."

Frank seemed to consider that. "Let me grab a tape measure."

Before I could argue, the Echo Watches blasted us out of Drake City and toward a really bad idea.

CHAPTER SEVEN

Winnemucca was super quiet. There were some cars navigating downtown, sure, but even on this Saturday night Dominic and I jaywalked without fear of getting run over. Once that glut of traffic passed, I expected tumbleweeds to roll by.

That's not to say there wasn't anything—a few shops, some bars and restaurants. Nice homes. We could walk to the other end of the town from the park in which we'd materialized without getting mugged, so, bonus.

I slung the backpack over one shoulder. "Thanks for dropping by my apartment first."

"Considering you would have whined about not having your supersuit, I didn't have much choice." Dominic kept his gaze resolutely away from mine.

"Relax. We'll take care of this. We always do." I hoped. Fingers crossed.

"Always? We've only fought as a team twice,

Mercury." Dominic sighed. "I use the term 'team' loosely."

"Only because you want to be in charge."

"I do have considerable experience the covert operations aspect of Procyon," he said. "For an architect, anyway."

"Sure. And my nighttime exploits killing monsters for the last couple of years doesn't count for jack."

"Will you stop it?" he snapped. "I'm trying to get us onto the same page, but your attitude's worse than usual. What is your problem? Besides an ingrown inability to play well with others."

"What's my problem?" I grabbed his shoulder so we both stopped in the middle of the sidewalk. Which was fine, because we were so far out the southwest end of Winnemucca, I was surprised there was paved highway, let alone a sidewalk. "Gee, let me think. I get dragged out of a perfectly normal day—"

"Mind-numbingly boring, was your description."

"*Normal*. Dragged out into a bachelor party that turns out awesome because, you know, *Europe*, and instead of ending up sleepy and full, I'm running away from my brother and the only guy who's ever cared about me like a real father should because you took us on a secret scavenger hunt for another stupid weapon that shouldn't even be on this planet!"

"This operation was necessary," Dominic said, "Unless you'd rather Serena Cyr bid the sword off to the richest criminals east of Berlin. And what if one of them was a doppelganger from the other Earth? Who knows what they could use the sword for?"

"The point is, I should have been in on the loop. Loredana, too."

"Alvarez was worried about your mental state lately."

"Mental state?"

"Yes. Distracted. Irritable."

I rolled my eyes. "Dominic, that is me literally since kindergarten."

"You know what I mean." He prodded my chest. "Something's been weighing you down, since we fought that fiery astral fiend."

"Astral fury."

"I don't care about the name! You haven't been fighting crime. Extradimensional incursions have declined, so you haven't been battling the evils of the Interstice, either." He folded his arms. "So, out with it. What's been bothering you?"

What an idiot. I pushed past him and kept walking. My target was a single-story former gas station of stucco and wood timbers. The paint had worn off its sign, leaving a ghost of "Conoco." Someone with a steady hand had painted "Trinkets Treasures Antiques" in bold blue letters in its place. "Three guesses. They all start with 'the wedding.'"

Dominic laughed, but when I didn't turn around, he jogged to catch up. "Are you serious? That's what's been bothering you? It's marriage, for heaven's sake, Mercury. It isn't the end of the world."

"That's not—I know that."

"But you and Loredana … You love her."

"Of course I do! I wouldn't have proposed if I didn't."

"And she loves you. Anybody who isn't blind and deaf can tell." He shook his head. "Look, all the stories, all the stereotypes—don't worry about those. The best thing for you is to find a woman who makes you happy, and who you make happy. Someone for whom you wouldn't hesitate to give your life. There will be conflicts. Probably more than you'd imagined outside of slaying monsters. But, well, as a certain book I revere says plainly, man wasn't meant to live alone."

I bit back a smart aleck response because, let's face it, I had those in heaps. "That's the problem."

"What is?"

"The …" I blew out a breath. I really wished I was having this conversation with anyone else. Or maybe, maybe he was the perfect guy. Younger. Married a few years. Semi-devout, from what I could tell. "The part the Bible talks about."

"What part? A man and a woman joining in marriage?" Dominic smiled. "Or the part about submitting?"

I chuckled. "No, uh … Sort of. It's the …" I rolled my hand. "The leaving and cleaving. Especially the cleaving. If you catch my drift."

"Oh." Dominic's eyes widened. "Oh. Wait a minute. Are you telling me you've never—?"

I held up a hand. "Don't."

"I'm not laughing. I'm serious." He ran a hand through his hair. "Wow. Mercury, I have to say, that's near miraculous."

"Yeah?"

"I mean, you are a nice-looking guy—"

"You're kinda hot yourself, Operative Gemini."

Dominic frowned. "This is serious, Mercury. Jess and I were young when we got married. Right at the end of college. So, abstaining wasn't too far-fetched, especially given the cultural expectations from both our families. But you …"

"I know. It's weird."

"I think it's commendable."

I winced. "Now you make it sound like I'm *really* lame."

"Hey. I understand why you're worried. But if you two haven't …" He repeated my hand-rolling motion. "Then you should look at this as a chance to express your love to each other. It is the kind of thing we aspire to in the sight of God."

"Okay. Thanks. I just don't want to, ah, you know. Be bad." I grimaced. Wow. That sounded terrible even to me.

Dominic chuckled. "I think you kids will be fine. What does Loredana think?"

"We … Haven't talked about it much. I mean, we're looking forward to the honeymoon, but, uh, we've been… Non-specific."

"You'd better remedy that. If you're having concerns, she needs to hear them. Because she may be thinking the same things."

"That's a lot of talking about feelings."

"Since you've got the heroic part of saving the world down pretty well, I'm sure you can fit some of that into your schedule."

Yeesh. A few months hanging around me and everyone's a comedian.

The store sign said closed, but as soon as we reached the front door of Treasures & Trinkets, a thirty-something woman of Native background I couldn't pin down opened it. Even set off jingly chimes. She was a hand taller than me, with black hair dangling clear to her waist, tied in a thick braid. Streaks of silver touched her temples. Two gold earring loops on each lobe and a tiny animal—wolf?—pierced her nose.

"You're it?" Her voice was firm but airy, like it had blown on the dust across the desert.

"If by it, you mean ready for battle, then yep." I held out my hand and grinned. "Mercury Hale."

She inspected my hand as if it were a scorpion and she were holding a shovel. When she reached for the door handle, the light overhead flickered across the violet tattoo of a pawprint on her right shoulder. Which I could see clearly, because she wore a blue and red flannel shirt sans sleeves with tight blue jeans that had suffered some tears.

"So, ah, Procyon called you, right?" I pointed beyond her. "You got an office back there? Or maybe a squad of security muscleheads?"

"Just me." Her smile was sort of welcome. I mean, she stopped frowning, but I also felt like Jerry when Tom cornered him outside the mouse hole. She zeroed in on Dominic. "And you're Gemini?"

"I—Yes. Dominic Zein." They shook hands. "Have we met?"

"Edith Pathkiller, and no, we haven't. But I keep up on the dossiers from headquarters. Too bad it became rubble—though I hear they got a bunker. Lovely." She headed back into the store. "Hurry up."

We hurried.

There wasn't a chance to peruse the tables and shelves full of knick-knacks. Plenty of old books, used typewriters, a handful of clocks, pottery, military surplus, postcards … Anything and everything you could imagine. Had a musty smell that surprised me, given that Winnemucca's dry air was itching the heck out of my eyes.

Edith led us behind the counter, with its stack of papers, Square payment console, and ancient cash register, into a short hallway. Emergency exit door at the back. Bathroom on the right—because where else would it be? There was another door across from it. A metal one. Bookshelves filled the wall to its left.

"I've got him tracked." Edith held her cell phone up to the bookshelf adjacent to the door. A red light flashed between two Zane Grey westerns. The shelf, two feet wide, rumbled back until it zipped to the left, revealing a closet full of computer monitor and glowing racks of equipment I'd only seen in Tracking.

"Secret passageway," Dominic murmured. "That's excellent."

"It'd be more excellent if it was another person with Medan weaponry," I said. "You wouldn't happen to have some of that, would you, Edie?"

"Edith." She sat in the lone chair and donned a wireless headset. "You two zip it. Looks like your compatriot is right on target. ETA five minutes."

I blinked. "That's—slightly faster than the 300 miles per hour I was quoted. I thought we still had a half hour or more."

"You'd better hope his powers don't have a long range."

"No kidding. So ... What's your plan?"

Edith drew back on a handle. The roof shuddered. Metal clanked overhead. "You boys get out front and be ready to intercept him."

"This just in: We can't fly."

"Don't worry about it. I'll get him down to you." She flicked her hands to the emergency door, eyes searching the radar screen at the center. A blinking red light sped toward the center of green concentric rings. "Go."

Dominic smacked my shoulder. I'd have smacked him back, but he was already on his way out the emergency exit. I sprinted after, into the rapidly cooling night air.

There he was. Above the eastern horizon—a glint of white streaking through the sky. Any other day, another threat, the sight would have made me pump my fists and let the bad guys know they were in deep trouble.

Problem was that Brandon was bringing that trouble to us.

"What are you doing out here?" Dominic put on the ski mask. The Echo Watches glowed under his sleeves.

"What? Oh." I ducked back to the restroom. Forgot all about getting into the tights.

Half a minute later, I was back outside—not that anyone could see unless they squinted. The pulsar stave's energies fed through the suit, making it indistinguishable from the crumbling adobe and hardscrabble prairie underfoot.

"That is a neat trick." Dominic watched the incoming rocket of a human. "I don't mind you knowing, I'm a bit nervous about this."

"Relax. Like I said, we took him before."

"Took? It was a draw. And he was being nice. This time, I doubt the people steering his mind are worried about our well-being."

I glanced back at the rooftop. Flat surface, except for a couple of ventilation pipes and a hulking swamp cooler that sat at an angle. "Just be ready. Whatever Edie in there has planned, I have a feeling we're gonna need you to focus on praying if Brandon decides to flex his muscles before I can poke him with the pulsar stave."

The ground around us started shaking. Chunks of concrete ripped free from the old gas pumps, drifting above our heads—so, not an earthquake. Check. And more to the point, the shaking and breaking was confined to an area that encircled the gas station alone. It didn't even bother the highway pavement.

Brandon slowed enough I could make out a human form, but it wasn't his costume. Duh. I figured he'd left that back in Drake City, because who takes a superhero suit of armor to a bachelor party? He still had on the ski mask but wore a winter coat over top.

"Okay." I backed up. "Here's the plan. I'll get a running start. Enhanced speed. You use your Echo Watches and—"

A growing hum interrupted my train of thought. The gleam from the antiques store's roof derailed that train and threw it off a cliff. That gleam belonged to a spotlight. First impression? The spotlight was way too heavy duty. It swiveled on a hydraulic mount as panels dropped away, panels I realized had been the sides of the swamp cooler, nothing more than a rusty shell concealing that thing.

The humming intensified. No glaring light. Just a pulse.

Wait. I'd seen that pulse before.

"What is it?" Dominic asked.

"The same kind of military-grade mounted laser turret Procyon used to fry a bunch of zombies downtown," I said.

Brandon must have realized something was up, even in his brainwashed state, because he raised his hands. His jacket erupted in fire. He hurtled to the ground, staggering in mid-flight, before skidding in a dusty heap toward is.

"Come on!" I ran for the road. "Here's hoping Edie didn't incinerate the poor guy!"

She hadn't. Brandon was on his feet, shedding the smoldering remains of his coat. He turned around just in time to see Dominic sprinting, his Echo Watches raised for attack.

Sure, Dominic could have teleported. But I needed a distraction.

I lunged for Brandon and slammed against the shielding he had in place. The suit didn't cut through it but whipping out the pulsar stave sure helped.

Not by much. I got six inches from that stupid medallion of his before an invisible force threw me fifty feet.

But Dominic, bless his uptight little heart, blasted right through the shield and sent Brandon tumbling.

I whipped the pulsar stave around—after I inverted myself so I wasn't laying around upside down—and contributed my own weapon to the fireworks display.

Also didn't hurt that a truck-sized patch of dirt exploded right in front of Brandon, lifting up a cloud that obscured everything he'd need to see.

I accelerated through the dust storm, draining power from the pulsar stave into my suit. A kick in the face was just what the doctor ordered, so I sprang up at Brandon using my prosthetic leg—you know, the one that could channel extradimensional energies through it.

Would've broke his nose good if he hadn't caught me.

I froze in midair, twisted twice, and slammed face first into the dirt.

Dominic was already there, pinned on his chest. He gasped through the dust swirling around him.

Couldn't imagine why. Probably because Brandon was using the medallion to squash us both. My fingers clawed at dirt. The pulsar stave was a foot away. Almost—Had it—

Suddenly air rushed back into our lungs. The invisible field let us go.

Brandon cocked his head, like a dog hearing one of those high-pitched whistles. Then he barreled by us so fast the wind rolled us over.

He bashed straight through the antiques store and out the other side, turning into a pile of rubble. Windows shattered. The ceiling collapsed. Walls crumbled.

His form rose into the evening sky, leaving a destroyed Procyon office with its guts spilling out the back, and two battered operatives literally eating his dust.

CHAPTER EIGHT

My first thought, after the haze cleared out, was, *We'd better get out of here before the police show up.*

My second thought? *Edie! Is she okay?*

Third? *Alvarez is gonna kill us if Brandon doesn't.*

Dominic helped me up. We were slathered head to foot in so much dirt we'd have no problem camouflaging ourselves if we went traipsing across the plains. Neither of us was up for the hike.

"You good?" My voice rasped like I'd spent way too long shouting in a nightclub. Or a coffee bar-slash-dance hall. Which was really where I would have rather been.

"Passable." Dominic swayed. I held his arm, but he shook free. "I'll be fine."

"Come on. Edie."

His eyes widened and he took off, though with a limp whereas before he'd hit a smooth stride.

Antiques were strewn about the sunbaked earth.

The dusty, worn treasures and trinkets we had passed in a blur before the fight were reduced to debris. I hoped Procyon hadn't spent too much out of their Operations budget to stock the place.

More importantly, I hoped they had backups for the sensitive tachyon array Tyrone Thomas was swooning over. But as I waded through the wreckage, I couldn't help but notice the lack of advanced electronics. Plenty of wiring befitting an old building.

Dominic lifted a wood beam aside. "Where is this tachyon array?"

"Great minds." I lifted a door that had been shattered in two. There was a heap of rubble to our left—the secret office, maybe. "Over here."

The debris shifted. A hiking boot slammed through. Edie shouldered the rest of the debris blocking her way. Aside from scrapes atop her shoulders and a bruise on her face, she looked unscathed. Which was great, considering how scathed I felt.

"Good try, but not good enough." She dusted herself off and slipped a backpack over her shoulders. Big old hiking bag, with patched holes. "Ready?"

"Ready for what?" I indicated the ruined store. "Don't you have sensitive information we need to gather up? Electronics that need to be dismantled?"

Smoke drifted from the crumpled metal box behind her. The whole office was armored, turned out, which explained why it hadn't blown apart when Brandon smashed through the building. "Molten slag in forty-five seconds," Edie said. "We'd better get to Drake City, though, if we're going to regroup."

"I'm sorry." Dominic held up his hand. "But Manager Alvarez at HQ would insist we ensure that the tachyon array is either secure or destroyed before we depart."

Sirens wailed from downtown Winnemucca. A fire engine's klaxon blared. "Yeah, and preferably fast," I said.

"Don't worry about it. It's been called a tachyon array for operational security but trust me, it's safe." She stepped over the rubble of her outpost like she was treading through cow pies. Even kicked aside a broken set of porcelain dishes. So … I didn't think she was attached to the contents of her store.

"Again, I'll need proof of that before we escape." Edie put her hands on her hips. The way her biceps tensed, I didn't think Dominic understood the full ramifications of irking that lady. "That's gonna have to wait, Operative Gemini, until somebody with higher clearance than a two-year freelancer who accidentally fell into our sights can muster. Get us teleported back to Drake City before we all have to spend the night in the luxury of Winnemucca's drunk tank."

Dominic started to say something, but I clapped my hands across his mouth and around the back of his head. "Shut up," I muttered, "And get beaming."

Because I wasn't looking forward to the next conversation any more than the rest of us.

⌘ ⌘ ⌘

The conference room at Procyon's Drake City office seemed smaller, even though we only had one extra person. I bet having Manager Hector Alvarez shouting at us from a big screen had something to do with it."

"This is outrageous! I expect a muck-up of this magnitude from Mercury, not you." Alvarez loomed over us from the safety of his desk on the other side of America. Given how short he was in real life, I couldn't take the looming seriously. Which is why I had my feet propped on the table and was leaned back enough so I could stare at the ceiling.

Dominic stood with his hands clasped behind his back. "Sir, with all due respect—"

I snorted.

"Who was that?" Alvarez asked.

I raised my hand.

"No one asked for your input at this point. You weren't read in on this operation."

"I'll add that to the list as Stupid Thing Number Two you did when it came to this plan," I said. "Number One being, you didn't tell Loredana."

"The decision to keep you both out of this operation was—"

"None of my business, I get it. Guess what? Still stupid." I looked around the table. "You let this group get involved in what should have been a simple snatch and grab. The consequence of compartmentalizing your intel? Big-time superhero got brainwashed by the bad guys."

"And you guys got stomped by him," Sean muttered. "Because *duh*."

"Why is there a high school student in a classified briefing?" Alvarez snapped.

"Personal connection to the case, Hector. He's a valuable witness with insight to Airfoil's psychological state." Tyrone winked at me, so subtly I don't think Alvarez noticed.

"And the man with the beard?"

"Frank Belasco."

I thought Alvarez was gonna need a new set of eyes when his were ready to pop clean from his skull. "Frank *Belasco*? Homeland will have us locked up in an unlisted detention center if word gets out he's inside one of our facilities, Tyrone!"

"Take it easy. We're locked down tight. And better yet, we brought Pathkiller in."

"Oh." Alvarez's color returned to its normal, not-enraged hue. "She's safe?"

Edie was using a military-grade knife to whittle a piece of wood. Where'd she get it, from the store's wreckage? It looked like a table leg. Shavings littered the stone brown carpet. "Right here, Mr. Alvarez."

"I apologize. I've never seen your image, Operative Pathkiller. I had no idea you were stationed in Winnemucca."

"They keep my whereabouts low key, except in emergencies." Edie raised an eyebrow, her smile as sharp as before. "Which, judging by how upset you boys all are, this qualifies as."

"Of course. Well, any assistance you can render would be helpful."

"You got it."

"Sir ..." Dominic raised his hand. What was he, in third grade? "About the tachyon array—"

Alvarez shook his head. "Tyrone, if you think this warrants it, read them in. Without Belasco and the boy."

"Understood. Happy trails."

"Yes. Excuse me while I assure the U.S. Air Force they don't need to shoot down a superhero."

Alvarez vanished from the screen. Tyrone dug out his wallet. He handed Sean a ten-dollar bill. "Vending machine's down the hall, around the corner to your right. Go crazy."

"Only if you don't charge a bazillion dollars for a Snickers." Sean took the money, though, and stalked by Frank.

"Sorry, Mr. Belasco. Kids only." Tyrone waggled his wallet.

"No problem. I'll check in with your techs about our weapons."

As soon as the glass door eased shut, Tyrone sat at the head of the table. "I'll make this easy to digest: Edith Pathkiller is the tachyon array."

I blinked a couple of times. Dominic held up his hand, finger raised as if to make a point, then shook his head.

"Not that helpful? I should be clearer. There is

no tachyon array. That's how it's recorded in all our files. Edith is the one providing insight on the where and when of potential rips between this dimension and the Interstice."

"She's in Forecasting?" Our San Camillo headquarters had been down a Forecaster ever since Marigold Yen had turned out to be evil and, well, disintegrated while trying to destroy Earth. But she threw great dinner parties that made me feel part of a true family before, you know, the evil.

"It'd be more accurate to say she *is* Forecasting. All of her visions precede what San Camillo and other offices experience."

"Dark stuff." Edie held the stick up to the ceiling lights. It had an edge that looked as sharp as her knife's. "Nothing you'd be able to sleep through after seeing."

"Why mislead us?" Dominic asked.

"To keep her existence a secret and keep her safe. That's been her family's way for generations, ever since Elijah Pathkiller wielded the pulsar stave in 1848."

I could feel the cold metal grow even frostier though the suit's fabric. Her ancestor had been there—the battle that determined the beginning of Procyon Foundation and its century-plus duty to protect our dimension.

"Six generations," Edie said. "I'd like that to continue."

"I bet. How can you help us now? We're not

dealing with astral fiends."

"My sensitivities extend to objects that draw their power from the Interstice."

"Meaning ..."

"Meaning I can sense their approach, from great distances, but also up close and fast."

I squinted at her. "Sounds like we can test that."

"Only if you want more bruises." She scraped a long peel off the stick with her knife.

Yikes.

"Suffice it to say, Ms. Pathkiller's going with you, because of the somewhat desperate circumstances involved." Thomas pulled a metal comb from his wallet and brushed at his beard as he continued, "Let's all do me a favor and not tell Hector. He'd have a stroke and I don't think the board wants to appoint a second new manager of the San Camillo office in less than a year."

"Don't tempt me with a Christmas gift," I muttered.

The new—or, I guess, modified old—weapon wasn't ready yet. I found myself with extra time and not a lot to do, besides be anxious, because while we were waiting, Airfoil was racing toward San Camillo and Serena had the rest of my friends on her airplane heading in the same direction.

Plus, it was late Saturday in a Procyon office, so besides Tracking and the lab, the place was deader than a recently slain astral fiend. But when my phone buzzed, I knew I needed to answer it.

<Alvarez contacted me. Urgent.>

Loredana.

I made the call.

"Mercury." Loredana's relief spilled from the phone. "Thank goodness you're unharmed."

"There was a little harm. No amputations, though, so I'm happy." I grimaced at the muscle cramp in my leg above where the prosthetic attached. None of the bruises would be visible in a few days. Advanced healing would take care of that. For now, though, they were painful reminders of failure. "Airfoil and company are headed to HQ."

"So I understand from Manager Alvarez. I assume they learned of our new location from Lieutenant Ramos?"

"Yeah. This mind control must allow Serena and her new BFF Xia access into the person's brain." I chuckled, though it was a weary sounding chuckle even to me. "Which makes it even better they didn't latch onto my brain."

"Quite. One can hardly fathom the level of distress your mad thoughts would inflict on them."

"How's L.A.?"

"Balmy. Lovely."

"You, ah, coming back in because of this?"

"I am."

"Sounds like a lousy reason to cancel your weekend."

"Crises are nothing new to me. I have already chalked up my impending absence to a work issue." I could imagine her smirk, the accompanying raised eyebrow.

"Sorry about that."

"Nonsense. This is the life I chose—the one to which I'm called. It took your reminder for me to rededicate myself."

"I'm glad I did, because Procyon would fall apart without you. There wouldn't be the Procyon we know, no matter who sits in the manager's office."

"Well." Her voice dropped in volume. "I wouldn't go so far—"

"Don't kid yourself, Loredana. You've put your life in danger as much as me, sans superpowers. That takes as much courage—probably more. Which is me saying, if you want to sit this one out, you should. Go off grid for twenty-four hours. I'm not saying we don't need you. It'll be weird without you shooting things while we're saving the world."

"I appreciate the sentiment, I do—assuming, of course, you're not making such a proclamation to keep me out of danger."

I laughed. "Are you serious? Maybe if I didn't think astral fiends were crying themselves to sleep somewhere whenever you showed up with me. No, I meant what I said. Think of it as your Christmas present and wedding gift wrapped up in one package."

"One assumes the ring is present enough, along with all it accompanies."

Well. I wondered if Procyon had dialed up the thermostat in this part of the building.

"I will consider your offer, love, but do not be astonished if I were to arrive at headquarters to greet our enemies," she said.

"I wouldn't bat an eye."

"Text me when you and your team reach their rendezvous."

"You got it."

"I love you, Mercury. Be safe."

All I could think about was her at her party with her friends, and me laughing up a storm with the guys—normal things that normal people who are about to get married do. Not wondering how to reschedule social engagements because brainwashed superheroes are trying to wreck a secret organization in charge of destroying monsters. "I love you, too."

The call ended. I tapped the edge of the phone against my lips.

Dominic leaned around the doorframe. "That sounded like it went well."

"Eavesdropping much?"

"I have made it one of my skills. Searching for doppelgangers from an alternate dimension gets easier when you learn how to listen in on conversations that the participants would rather I didn't hear."

"Your mom must be proud."

Dominic made a face. "Prouder than Father, if either knew what I was doing."

Sore subject, apparently. "What's up?"

"We're wanted down in the tech lab. Frank's getting geared up. Oh, and ..."

I thought Dominic was right behind me as I headed for the elevator, but I had to stop. "And?"

"I can't see why you're worried." He smiled. "From what I heard, you two trust each other a great deal more than a lot of couples I know, and there's no barrier to honesty. I wish Jess and I had been that mature in how we communicated at the beginning."

I bet that was the first time I'd ever heard anyone use the M-word about me. "Thanks, Dominic."

"So, when it comes to the wedding night, and the honeymoon, you'll be much better off if you communicate clearly what—"

"And we are so done here." I skipped the elevator and pushed through the emergency door to the stairwell before he could finish his latest advice.

Footsteps slapping on concrete told me he was right behind, and by the time we emerged on the fifth floor and walked to the lab, he was side by side with me. Grinning like an idiot.

"You could have at least got me a present," I said. "Make the evening worthwhile before it blew up."

"Are you serious? Did you see the menu prices? At the restaurant in *Paris*?" He shook his head, still grinning. "I barely know you from Adam."

"That doesn't mean ..." I lost the rest of my sentence when the opaque frosted glass doors to the lab slid open. "Wow."

"I mean ... It certainly is." Dominic scratched at

his chin.

The "wow" was reserved for the hulking figure at the center of the room, and I don't mean Bruce Banner's alter ego. It looked like a mad scientist had crossed a lion with a gorilla, fed it steroids, then turned it into a headless robot. Slate gray metal covered every inch, except where powerful pistons and hydraulics acted as artificial muscles. It sat on its haunches, front legs a foot longer than the back ones. A motor or other power source rumbled, smooth and low, not like a combustion engine.

"No visible weapon," Dominic said.

"That's because we're attaching it." Frank pushed long tubular weapon on a thick-wheeled cart, the gun suspended on chains. The front half of the weapon looked old—dented, scarred. The rest seemed as new as if they'd ordered the parts off Amazon.

"The tachyon weapon should distort any similar source it's fired at." Tyrone leaned on a nearby worktable. He gestured at a pair of young techs in white lab coats bearing Procyon insignia. They hustled to the robot's side.

"Are you sure it'll do the trick?" I asked.

"Since Airfoil himself brought us the prototype after being slapped around by it twice, yes, I think it'll do the trick."

Frank backed away as the techs wheeled the gun into position. Sean sidled up to him, chewing on the last chunk of a Snickers bar.

"Must be tough for you," I said. "Got your action

in during the Drake City siege and now a robot gets to play in your place."

"Good thing it's not a robot." Frank crossed to the side of the machine and clambered up its side. I'd missed the handholds behind its shoulders. He pried open a hatch like a DeLorean's car door.

A narrow, dark slit lit up with instrumentation. Screens. And controls.

"What do you think?" Frank patted the armored hide like he'd finally found the perfect puppy. "Should clear the ceiling in your loft, right, Mr. Zein?"

"No way," I muttered. "Dominic wrecks my bachelor party and this guy gets a BattleMech."

CHAPTER NINE

Given the size of Bruno—that's what Frank insisted we call his new mech toy—it made the most sense for us to travel by portal in groups. Dominic beamed himself and Frank out of the lab, which left me pacing while Sean ate yet another Snickers.

"Don't gimme that look," he said through a mouthful of nougat.

"What look? My mask is down."

"The parent look. Like I'm gonna ruin my dinner 'cause I've had like two candy bars."

"It's four, kid."

"Whatever." He wiped his mouth with the back of his hand.

I mouthed, *Whatever*, in sing-song fashion when my head was turned. I lifted the mask up. Too hot in the lab, especially while pacing.

Easy, Mercury, I told myself. *Leave the kid alone. His dad's in trouble.*

Kind of like yours is.

No way. Couldn't let myself think about Ramos. If I did, it'd be impossible to focus on the coming fight. It was gonna be tough as it was trying to avoid hurting Teget, who was my equal in terms of skill and strength. Ramos was an even tougher call.

One wrong move, and I could kill him.

Dominic flashed back into the lab. The techs scurried after loose reports. Geez, guys, stretch the budget for some paperweights.

"Ready?" Dominic held out his hand.

"I'll stand real close instead, thanks." I budged up against him. "On my count."

He shook his head. "That isn't how this works."

"Whatev—" Huh. I sounded way too much like Brandon's kid. "Okay then. Ready."

Dominic dialed up the Echo Watches. The world blurred and distorted.

And a body slammed into my ribcage.

It wasn't fun to be frozen in space-time, hurtling through the portal but somehow also stationary, while stabbing pain rocked the same bruises I was trying to heal. It wasn't until we emerged in Dominic loft that I realized the source of the pain was a stupid teenager untangling himself from our limbs.

Sean whooped like he'd witnessed the winning run of the World Series. "Awesome! So awesome!"

Not fair. He wasn't even queasy.

"Are you out of your mind?" Dominic snapped. "You could have killed us all! Or worse!"

"I'm gonna regret asking." I pinched my eyes shut and tried my best to not vomit. "But what's worse?"

"Getting us trapped between dimensions."

"What's that like?"

"I have no idea and I don't want to experience it." Dominic raised a finger at Sean. "You stay right here. Procyon security will be along to get you on a flight back to Drake City—"

"No, they won't! I'm coming with you guys. This is my dad we're talking about. Frank thinks he can blow some stuff up and that'll fix everything."

"Wasn't he your idea?" I muttered.

"Yeah, but, okay, he's not always stable."

"And this is the guy we let ride a mech gorilla," I whispered to Dominic.

Sean grit his teeth. "Frank will fight until he's dead, and that's great on our side, but Dad's against us right now and … I think I can talk him back. Out of it."

"No. Not a chance." Dominic pushed Sean toward the kitchen. "You stand over here."

A flash of light made us both blink. Then came a few more.

"Let me go with you," Sean said, "Or I'm posting these."

When he said, "These," he meant photos of me and Dominic standing in the loft's living room, our faces unmasked.

"You wouldn't dare."

Sean narrowed his eyes. His thumb hovered over

the Instagram button.

"Give me that!" Dominic reached for him.

"Hey, whoa, take it easy." I got between them and had to push Dominic back toward the center of the loft. "Let's bring the kid. Keep him back out of harm's way."

"How do you have any idea where safety is? With Airfoil in the loose—"

"My dad is *not* on the loose! I can help him!"

I whistled. Two fingers in the mouth and everything. Huh. I didn't know I could do that. "Will you two shut up? Sean, you're right, he's your dad. Quit whining. We'll take you, but so help me, if Brandon uses a gravity field to smash you into hummus, I'm not scooping up your bits and mailing them back to whoever your grandparents are."

Dominic smiled, but I got in his face before he could activate Full Gloat. "And you, quit giving orders like you've got seniority. This is our mess; We're going to clean it up. But I'm calling the shots, because so help me, I'm going to salvage *something* awesome out of this ruined night!"

Neither had quippy comebacks or even snide rejoinders. All they gave me were oddly similar sulky looks. Funny how much a 30-something married professional could resemble a teenage brat.

I pointed. "Portal. Now."

We circled up, a sullen trio. Sean held his breath as the bubble of light expanded. He stared at the forested slope beyond.

Mount Shasta.

Our entry blew the pine needles off every conifer in a twenty-foot radius. I squinted up at the setting sun. Its golden circle lounged on the other side of the towering peak, spilling its colors on the scattered snow. I blew out a feather of breath. Chilly up here, but not terrible. I let the pulsar stave send heat through the suit's channels.

"It's a decent vantage point." Dominic lifted the black mask up from his neck, covering the bottom of his face all the way to the bridge of his nose. He zipped up his jacket and pointed. "Up there, from the northeast."

"Yeah, I got it. Hand me your phone."

The tachyon dowser routed its sensor information to the phone's screen. A basic 2-D map of the region showed Brandon as a red blinking light. Incoming, for sure. "Hang on," I said. "What about the plane?"

"Dropped off radar while you guys were fooling around in Winnemucca." The voice pierced through static on my earbud.

I winced and rubbed at the side of my head. "Frank? You stop off for a bite somewhere?"

The hillside shuddered underfoot. Bruno stomped into our clearing, battering branches. The tachyon gun pulsed with purple lightning.

"You brought Sean?" Frank's sigh sent the earbud into another round of static. "Great plan. Procyon has some funny ideas about the rules of engagement. What about Pathkiller?"

The tops of Dominic's cheeks darkened. "I'll, ah, be right back."

He flashed out.

"Seriously? He forgot her?" Sean dissolved into laughter.

"Shut up, okay? Shut. Up." In all fairness, I'd forgotten, too. But there were getting to be more bodies on this team than I could reasonably be expected to remember. Made me long for the days I worked solo.

"I'll get into position," Frank said. "Once I bring him down, it'll be up to you to hold him down so I can pound him."

"Yeah, I figured. That's what we did at Winnemucca, though, and it didn't turn out as well."

"Strength in numbers, Mercury. He's drastically outnumbered."

"That didn't seem to stop him when you guys faced down a mercenary army."

"None of them could disable his powers."

I checked the tachyon dowser. Only a few minutes remaining. Still just a single dot. "Hey, you said the plane fell off radar. How's that possible? No way Serena got her hands on a stealth aircraft."

"The crews at Rampart's airport said it looked like a Learjet or the equivalent. My guess it has a reflective coating, or maybe active jamming. Either way, Procyon tells me the signal shrank until it was no bigger than a goose. Drones are up looking for it."

"You caught up really fast on the intelligence of

an organization that doesn't like you very much."

"Tyrone's all right. He owes me, in any case." The mech stomped out of our clearing, heading further up the slope, where the trees thinned out. "Don't screw up."

"Thanks. Great pep talk."

I stood there, hands on my hips, not sure if any of this was a wise idea. That plane could be in San Camillo by now, leaving Teget ready to wreak some havoc of his own, but splitting up our forces could be a bad idea.

Security could handle my brainwashed brother and a cop. Without killing them, though?

Dominic rematerialized, this time with Edith Pathkiller. She wore a heavy woolen long coat with fur fringe, and she had—a bow.

"Seriously?" I mimicked firing a tiny arrow.

"If it was good enough for my grandfather, it's good enough for me."

To be fair, it was made of a thick, sturdy wood with Native symbols carved on the arms. Very cool looking. And the arrows she carried were modern, I assumed fiberglass and metal. Against someone like Airfoil …

"Incoming," Frank said.

He could have been calling for a drizzle on the Weather Channel. But Bruno hunkered against the mountainside, reared up on its hind legs, and fired.

A purple, jagged streak crackled across the sky. Brandon whipped around it, angling toward the ground.

A second burst came closer, but this weapon was no laser—it moved way slower than the speed of light. Bruno sidestepped, with Frank maneuvering the mech for what must have been a better angle.

"Get back." I pressed Sean behind me.

He slipped under my elbow. "If Dad can see me—"

"Okay, you know what?" I soaked in the energies of the pulsar stave and scooped him up under one arm. I whipped across the ground at high speed, vaulting toward one of the tallest trees that was back a good hundred feet from the clearing, but still visible from where we were making our stand. "Sit tight."

Then I left him sixty feet up, clinging between heavy branches and swearing in a way I was sure his dad would ground him for.

A screeching filled the clearing. Bruno's front arms tore off. They pinwheeled to either side. And a rift opened in front of the mech, a miniature canyon that grew by a foot every second.

"You'd better get clear, Frank!" I hollered.

"One second ..." Steady breathing filtered through my earbud's static.

Bruno let off a huge blast from the weapon, enveloping Brandon in a purple shower of sparks and lightning. He skidded along the mountainside, trying to get up in the sky again.

"Mine." Edie drew back her bowstring. An arrow sliced through the air so fast I never saw it—but I did see the burst of gold-tinged light that exploded at Brandon's chest, forcing him to shield his face. The same light rippled up and down the arms of her bow.

Medan, maybe?

"Go." I grabbed Dominic's arm.

He teleported us to his loft—the temperature change made my skin tingle even under the full supersuit. Then we slingshotted ourselves back to Mount Shasta, six feet from where Brandon was tottering upright.

I planted the pulsar stave dead center to his chest.

He shouted. The air around us rippled. Dominic was thrown end over end, scraping a through four inches of snow mingled with dirt and rocks.

I dug in, bracing myself against a boulder.

Brandon grasped the pulsar stave, its yellow sparks writhing around his hands and mine. I wasn't about to get dragged into a superhero version of tug-of-war, so I geared the weapon up for a blast. "Sorry, man, but this is gonna sting," I murmured.

Purple light enveloped us.

Brandon and I broke apart. I felt like I'd come out of the worst flu ever—no strength. Not even a bit of get up and go that I'd have as a normal guy. Drained. Good news? My opponent was in the same state.

Frank. He'd managed to get off another shot from Bruno, even with the mech collapsed on its side in the huge trench Brandon had dug. But the power levels on the attached weapon flickered and died. Guess that option was off the table for the next few minutes.

I tackled Brandon.

We grappled for control—him trying to wrest the pulsar stave out of my cold but not yet dead hands, me ripping at the front of his jacket for the medallion. I could feel the lump beneath the fabric; A touch of its frigid surface, even under clothing, set my teeth chattering.

I pulled him upright. He rammed my backside into the boulder, which I'd bet did wonders for my spine. I could see his eyes in the ski mask's openings—hazel, and aimless.

"Snap out of it!" I said. "You're the superhero, not me."

A tree branch walloped him across the back of the head. Brandon staggered away, our connection broken.

I felt the air wrinkle around us.

Oh, no.

"Down!"

A flash of yellow-white energy caught him in the left shoulder and his upper chest, spinning him around. Dominic slipped and slid down through the snow, an Echo Watch searing with light around his right wrist

The sudden attack gave me a clear view of the branch assailant—Sean, his jacket and jeans riddled with pine needles. "Dad!" he cried. "It's me! Come on, Dad!"

Brandon froze, hunched over. His lips moved, but the only sound was a hoarse, indistinct whisper.

"What'd he say?" Frank was thirty feet away, with a Ruger pistol aimed at Brandon. At his *head*.

"Don't shoot him! He's trying to speak." I waved Frank back.

"Excuse me for not being trusting." Frank sidestepped for a better aim.

"Hey! No!" Sean got into the line of fire. He put his hands on Brandon's arms. "Dad? Dad, wake up."

Brandon straightened. He put his shoulders back, and his stance became more relaxed, yet more—athletic, I guess. Almost graceful. His whisper was louder and, unfortunately, I could make out one word.

"*Mercury ...*"

"Oh, no," Dominic murmured.

Yeah. That sing-song cadence I never wanted to hear again but kept haunting me from the other side of the Interstice. Feminine and masculine, rolled into an overlapping array of tones. Marigold Yen, merged with Alexander Arkwright, all wrapped up in the strident, smooth, insistent voice of the Whisperer.

Apparently, they'd graduated to possession via ancient tiny robots. Awesome.

"Get out of him," I snarled, "Or I'll beat you into the next dimension."

"I don't think that will happen without this vessel's death," the voice said. "In front of his child? You would slay him? I know you're not the monster here."

I heard metal click.

Sean shouted an indistinct warning. A gunshot rang out. Brandon's head snapped back, but I didn't see blood, and overhead, wood splinters sprayed.

"You tried to kill him! You almost shot him!" Sean flailed at Frank, who held him at bay with one arm, while keeping his gun—from which smoke was drifting—far away.

"Someone had to," he snapped. "I would have taken him down if you hadn't fouled me up. You don't understand. No one else can get their hands on the medallion. And I mean no one. Would you rather I let the Garrison handle it? Or worse, allow them to apply a truce and let the Ashen clean up?"

Another blast of light sent Frank sprawling, his gun discarded, into the patchy snow next to where Brandon lay. I ducked down and checked on them both. Good. Breathing. I glared at Dominic. "Are you nuts? Quite trying to stun everyone!"

Dominic shook his head, gaze fixed on the other side of the clearing, both Echo Watches raised.

Teget stepped atop Bruno, brandishing his ax. The ski mask obscured his face, but I could read his body just as well—tense, energies pent up, ready for battle.

Ramos was with him, an M4 rifle aimed at me.

And Xia, the one guiding them, waved the black sword high above her head. A swirl of the symmachites stirred around Brandon.

You know what would have been nice? If Edie, the one who was supposed to be a better Forecaster than even Marigold, had foreseen any of this. Or was anywhere nearby. She'd evaporated like water on a hot sidewalk. Why'd Alvarez been in such awe of her?

If she had a great plan in mind, she hadn't shared.

Fine. I'd take care of it.

"Sean," I said. "Run."

The kid sprinted for the trees as bullets and light ripped between us.

CHAPTER TEN

The biggest problem wasn't the headache squeezing my brain. It was picking targets.

Because when the shooting started, Ramos' volley was the signal for a bunch of Syndax soldiers in forest camouflage to open fire from among the trees.

I sneered. At least I knew what to do about them.

Sean skidded on snow, arms flapping like he could decelerate with them. Dominic flashed into being between him and the nearest Syndax mercs and wrapped him in a bear hug. They vanished, leaving the Syndax guys rubbing their eyes.

Made it harder to see me when I landed the pulsar stave on the ground between them, a blast of its energy flipping them high over my head. They slapped off tree trunks en route back to Earth.

Frank had dragged Brandon to the shelter of the fallen Bruno, but that didn't stop the symmachites from swirling toward him, eager to reclaim their pawn. Frank leveled his pistol.

"Don't do it!" I shouted.

He just scowled and fired three rounds.

A Syndax soldier sneaking up behind me dropped, his goggles shattered.

"Oh." I whipped the pulsar stave around in time to block Teget's ax. "Hey, bro. Ready for a family chat?"

He wasn't listening. Or watching. None of that impeded his fighting skill, because he hammered at me with a ferocity he never exhibited on the few occasions we'd sparred.

So, I didn't feel bad about ducking a blow and whacking the back of his knee with the stave.

Ramos' advanced on Bruno, firing in measured bursts, never exposing himself to Frank's shots.

Light exploded behind Xia. Dominic's Echo Watches blazed at her, but she deflected with the sword before closing in on our architect turned operative. She swung down with her sword so hard I thought she was gonna slice off Dominic's arm, but the Echo Watch absorbed the impact. Sparks lit up their circle.

Brandon twitched. The symmachites were retaking him. I could see his limbs going rigid. If Frank had a plan, now was the time, because I was too busy spinning out of the reach of Teget's ax. It shattered tree branches inches from my ribs.

Frank ripped open Brandon's shirt. His fingers hovered over the medallion, a funny battered oblong piece of metal.

"Do it!" I broke the pulsar stave in half and battered Teget aside.

He grabbed the medallion.

A pulse of—well, nothing I could see kicked up pine needles, snow, and dirt throughout the entire clearing. Teget and I tumbled into each other, branches scratching our faces. Ramos rebounded off Bruno's metal hide. Dominic spun toward a tree but blinked out, leaving Xia to smash face-first into a fir.

Frank hovered in the midst of the mess, arms outstretched, fists clenched.

For a guy who spent his time shooting and driving a mech, he looked way too comfortable with that medallion between his fingers.

Xia, blood flowing from her nose, pointed with her sword and shouted. Eight Syndax soldiers emerged from the woods, rifles trained on Frank.

He swooped into their midst so fast I swore he was in two places at once.

Gunfire erupted all around him, but he was quick with the same kind of shields Brandon used. Bullets made like summer sparklers, their remnants digging a trench around him.

Frank snapped his right hand aside, like he was swatting a fly. Eight guns crumpled like tinfoil. Then he clenched his fist.

Eight legs *crunched*.

The soldiers collapsed in near unison, screaming. Blood seeped through pant legs.

Wow.

"It's always a kick, the way you guys see something that baffles your mind and immediately shoot at it." Frank's voice had a new, sharper edge to it, like he'd decided chewing on rocks would be tasty. "Even when phenomenal power explodes in your face, you think you have a chance."

He flexed his fingers. The soldiers rose off the snow, arms pulled away from their sides. Pulled too far, I realized because they shouted at the pain being inflicted.

"Like plucking leaves," Frank muttered.

"Hey, whoa, wait a second!" I whacked Teget across the face with the pulsar stave. Blood smeared the metal. Sorry, man, but I had to get out in front of this. I leapt away from him and underneath the ring of tortured soldiers. "Frank! Put them down. They're out. I need your help with the rest."

"Who? Ramos?" Frank flicked his fingers to the right.

Ramos tumbled like discarded paper on a windy street. He collided with Xia. Dominic teleported out of his way.

"I said, knock it off!" I blasted at his chest.

Frank dodged, but the pulsar stave's energy made him stutter step out of the air, near enough I could grab his ankle. I tore him the rest of the way down, slapping him into the melting snow and muddy ground.

An invisible blow—kind of felt like getting drop-kicked by an elephant—threw me against Bruno. Pain lanced up my back and down my legs.

"I'll kill every last one of them so they get it through their thick skulls they shouldn't mess with the Garrison." Frank raised his hands. Everyone in the clearing, including me and Dominic and even the disabled Brandon, floated. "That means you, too, if you're against me."

Something whistled past my head. I caught a flash of silver trailing yellow sparks right before a beach ball-sized supernova erupted against Frank's chest. His face went slack with shock, leached of color, and he collapsed.

I forced power from the pulsar stave through the suit and propelled myself toward him in a blink—so fast, in fact, I caught him in mid-stagger. I pulled the medallion from his fingers.

"What—?" Tears brimmed around dark brown eyes. He took in his surroundings. "I—it took over, didn't it."

"Won't lie, you went kind of crazy." I helped him stand.

He broke free. "There's a reason I couldn't do that anymore. Why they took my medallion away. The body gets old, worn, and the mind ..."

Dominic reappeared. "That went bad quickly. What happened?"

"Forget that." I glanced behind me. Edie stood atop Bruno, another arrow nocked. Her eyes gleamed with a subtle violet, not unlike the Syndax soldiers when they were hopped up on Arkwright's tachyon infusion. "Nice shot."

"We're not through this yet." She gestured with the bow.

Okay, so all the soldiers were down, but Teget was upright again, and Xia had retrieved the sword. Ramos knelt in the snow, immobile. Maybe Xia had put him on standby. Brandon was stiff as a board, though by the way his chest rose and fell, he was still alive.

Through the branches, though, I could see more camouflaged forms advancing.

"Nope, definitely not a trap," I muttered. "Here comes Round Two."

"I'll get Brandon to safety," Dominic said. "And get him to his son. I dropped Sean with Liz back at Procyon."

Xia advanced on us with the sword, Teget joining her with his ax. "Do it," I said, but as soon as Dominic reached Brandon, I realized my mistake. "Wait, Dominic! The bots!"

He was already leaning over Brandon and recoiled when I shouted. Too late. A stream of the symmachites poured from Brandon's face, surrounding Dominic's head. He swiped wildly and even blasted with the Echo Watches with inches of his nose.

I couldn't help him, though, because Frank was a shuddering mess and I had two crazed people with sharp weapons ready to take my head off.

They came at me simultaneously, Teget high, Xia low. Had to admit—for a lady who'd just picked up the dark sword, she was handling it like a pro.

I flung myself through the gap between them, using the pulsar stave's halves to deflect their strikes. I spun around, lashing through the air, not worried much about collateral damage to Xia but still pulling my punches with Teget.

Give me a break. I had him lined up to be my best man.

Right. Wedding. Funny the things that race through your brain when your busy fighting for your life. Reservations for Saito-on-sky were set. They'd better be set. My salary couldn't take it.

The Syndax soldiers stormed into the clearing. Super. Eight more. Didn't these guys have a supply problem when it came to recruits? How'd they find more people, anyway? Serena struck me as one of those LinkedIn types.

Arrows streaked by. With each dazzling explosion, soldiers fell, but the counterattack didn't prevent them from shooting.

Edie was on one knee, drawing, nocking, aiming, shooting with a grace and precision that made me think she was programmed to do what she was doing. She never missed. I mean, never, not even when gunfire tracked toward her.

Gunfire that sparked into the ground before the bullets could reach her, less than a foot from her face.

Brandon. His ski mask was gone, red hair a blazing beacon against the dreary mountainside, and there was blood trickling from a cut on his forehead.

He stood over Frank, invisible shield protecting the still hunker-over man and Edie at the same time.

Dominic was gone.

Which I figured was bad.

Xia slashed at me, but she got too manic for a couple seconds, which gave me an opening to pop her on the chin with the pulsar stave. A tooth flew loose. Talk about satisfying.

"You're kinda messed up. Ready to call it quits?"

She glared at me. "I won't let you take these gifts away from me. I'm not losing anything else."

"Yeah, I bet you're gonna lose a lot, fair warning."

More bad news? Teget roared a new challenge and threw himself on me. Next thing I knew, we rolled through the snow as the ax jabbed way too close to my face over and over again. Didn't help that the Syndax soldiers must have realized I was a prime target, because some of their shots kicked up snow near my legs.

I fired a blast or two their direction, tricky to manage while wrestling with a brainwashed Medan warrior but, hey, I managed. Probably winged one of them, judging by the shouts.

Brandon swooped overhead. He landed behind the soldiers, bullets flinging off him the whole way. His arms lifted, like he was catching an invisible load. A ramp of earth and snow tore loose and curled like a giant roll of carpet atop the Syndax crew. It smothered them up to their waists and chests, depending on how they'd been standing.

Teget's ax sliced along my shoulder, the bladed edge tearing the suit. I yelled in surprise at the pain burning there, smelled the blood. My blood.

Teget hollered again, but his war cry came upgraded with a stream of symmachites. They bypassed my mask, which sealed in my face, and dove right for the wound.

Talk about agony. Waves of fire rippled out from the wound, clear to my fingertips, and coursed throughout every cell. I could feel it seizing control. Muscles wouldn't obey. Couldn't keep my grip on the pulsar staves. Couldn't—

It wasn't so bad.

I relaxed. I mean, come on. I was getting married in a few days. Why worry about these guys? The nagging pressure on my mind crashed like a tidal wave across every anxiety. See? Even Teget was helping me up. And Dominic reappeared, standing beside us. Okay, so the Xia lady was waving her sword around too, and Brandon wouldn't stop shouting, but was it really that bad?

Xia didn't think so. Neither did Serena.

Or whoever was whispering to me.

Good. Join Dominic and the others. You're ready to reduce Procyon to rubble. Don't let anyone else's words sway you ...

Procyon. The new headquarters, underground. Dominic had taken Brandon's son Sean there, to hang out with Liz—to be safe. From what?

From us?

The pulsar staves vibrated with a tense, jarring sensation that rattled my hands and shook my arms. Awful as I was, I couldn't let go, even though I really wanted to. I tried to. Even smashed them against a tree. That just broke the tree.

The buzzing reached my head and I screamed.

The soothing wave evaporated.

Freaking symmachites!

I stopped fighting the vibrations and let them travel through the rest of me. My vision cleared. Things started moving again—things like Edie's arrows, which arced straight for my chest.

I crossed the pulsar stave and blocked them.

The nova burst blinded me worse than emerging from a darkened theater into the sunniest day imaginable. Teget, Dominic, and Xia screamed. So did Ramos.

Heck, even I joined in, at the same time I rejoiced in being freed.

When the light faded, and the buzzing in my ears subsided, I was left on my hands and knees. Still had the staves. Which, thankfully, had stopped buzzing.

I stared. Wondered if they were gonna start talking to me—because, after the Hedron of Orbits had gone sentient and tried to destroy San Camilo, nothing would have surprised me.

Except maybe Dominic looping his arm around Xia's waist and then doing the same to Teget.

They flashed away, leaving me reaching for their afterimage amidst a swirl of swirl of pine needles.

Someone yelped. That would be the Syndax soldiers. Brandon finished wrapping them up in the roll of dirt. Very Tom and Jerry, again.

"I take it you're okay." I brushed grime off the suit. It was gonna need a serious laundering.

"I'd be better if none of these guys had seen my face." He stayed behind the roll of dirt, out of the soldiers' line of sight, until he could fashion a bandit's mask for the lower half of his face from a jagged scrap torn off his jacket sleeve. "Where did they go?"

"Procyon." Edie leapt down from Bruno.

"And you know this because …?" I motioned for her elaborate.

"Because I know it. I see it." The purple tinge remained in her eyes. "We just have to get there."

"Then you two had better get Frank back on his feet." I pointed.

Frank was, technically, already on his feet, but by the way he braced himself against Bruno, you'd think he'd gotten home from a terrible bender. Dark circles had formed under his eyes and he was still too pale to be healthy.

"Frank?" Brandon whipped over to him. He held Frank's shoulders. "Where have you been? Did you—the medallion—?"

"Not now. We have to get to Procyon." Frank's voice shook, but he cleared his throat, and when he spoke again, the tremor was gone. "Sean's there."

Brandon swore. "Let's go, then."

"I'm sorry, but Ramos doesn't look fit to travel."

I pulled Ramos along. He trudged through the snow, his eyes unfocused, his mouth spilling indecipherable Spanish phrases. "Hang on a sec."

I pressed the pulsar stave into his hands.

The same keening pitch rose, my body vibrating in sympathy. Ramos' back arched as symmachites spilled from his mouth, eyes, and nose—but a golden glow obliterated them as they attempted to escape.

"I hope they're all screaming." Brandon's tone was as cold as the weather.

"Me too."

Ramos finally fell into my arms. He was drenched with sweat. "*Dios*," he murmured. "I thought—I prayed for them to depart. You don't know how I fought them …"

"I've got a pretty good idea." I couldn't resist a bear hug. My eyes stung. Probably pollen. "Welcome back."

He nodded, seeming embarrassed. Of course, if I'd taken potshots at my partners after losing control to tiny evil robots, I'd be chagrined in a big way.

"Good. Load up." Frank climbed into Bruno.

Edie followed him. "We'll take the landing pad first."

"How do you—?" I shook my head. "Never mind. Get Ramos inside, too."

It was a tight squeeze, with me and Edie helping Ramos clamber up on shaky legs. Those two crammed in with Frank made the Apollo capsule seem roomy.

"Guess that means I'm hanging on for dear life."

I scratched the back of my neck.

"Don't worry." Brandon lifted Bruno into the air, with as much apparent effort as me picking up a suitcase. "I won't drop you. Promise."

CHAPTER ELEVEN

Okay. I had no idea why Brandon played librarian during the day instead of soaring as Airfoil all the time. I guess he needed a job like everyone else.

But if I were him, I'd fly off and never come down.

We hurtled across the sky. I really hoped nobody was paying attention. Because they would have seen a guy in a winter coat flying toward the coast with a metal monstrosity dragged beneath and a man suited all in black with glowing yellow lines crisscrossing his outfit. Sure, I could have gone invisible, but A.) that would not have helped the rest of our team, and B.) I wanted to conserve our energy.

San Camillo curved around a long, narrow bay where the California coastline took several sharp turns. Forests clung to ravines and rolling hills north of the sprawling city grid. Fields and orchards spread east along the 311 winding out through the Arbor Valley.

I pointed for Brandon, who banked us into a steep dive. I cheered, arms spread wide like I was Peter Pan. No reason I should have trusted Brandon to keep me airborne but the guy's secrets weren't gonna ruin the moment for me.

Shouts trickled through Bruno's hatch. Couldn't tell who was unhappy with our ride but I would have put money on Ramos.

Brandon descended in a tight spiral until we were a few miles north of Procyon's hidden base, then skirted ten feet above treetop height the rest of the way in. A clearing suddenly spread before us, one I recognized as hidden in the woods from prying eyes. No aircraft present. I didn't see a V-22 Osprey whirling overhead, either, which meant the pilot on loan from the Chicago office was either off on a mission or had gone back to his home city.

The only plane was a white model with black wings edged in red, absent identifying marks. Didn't even carry registration numbers. What it did have were a set of turbofans inset in the wings to complement the jets at the tail. The concrete underneath was clean of dirt, indicating the plane had set down vertically.

Figured. Procyon's secret location lacked a runway, mostly because no one wanted to dig up the old missile silo covers that littered the clearing. A stubby bunker of weathered, pitted concrete hunkered at the far end. Other than that, the base left zero imprint.

"Frank?" Brandon shouted the question, I assumed into a radio. "Ready to drop. You have a prefer-ence as to where?"

The answer left Brandon shaking his head. "Okay, hang on."

He released the mech.

"Hey!" I yelped. "That thing doesn't come with a parachute, does it?"

"Landing gear, or so he says!"

Bruno was forty feet up when Brandon dropped it. The mech hit the ground once, bounded, up over the airplane, then skidded through the dirt. Metal feet dragged trenches.

Right on cue, Syndax soldiers spewed from the airplane.

Brandon and I landed beside it. "Hold still," he said.

Bullets exploded as fireworks around us. Hooray for invisible shields, I guess. "Those are awesome, but if you want me to take them out, I'll have to stop hiding behind you."

"You get the ones from the bunker."

The what?

He wasn't kidding. A half dozen more burst from the metal doors guarding the way into Procyon. Where did Serena hire all those henchmen? "Geez, guys, get real jobs," I muttered as I sped into their midst. And no, the irony of me using my extradimensional weapon as I complained weren't lost on me.

Brandon pummeled the soldiers who'd disembarked the airplane with ease. First, he tossed them like discarded toys. Then he used their guns as handcuffs or ankle binders. A couple guys hemmed him in close enough to land punches. Or try to. Brandon laid them out fast.

I'd wondered what Frank was waiting for when Bruno thundered past us, past the soldiers, and plowed through the airplane. Windows shattered. The fuselage ripped apart, shedding leather seats, their stuffing, and all kinds of wires. The back end of the plane tipped forward, sans landing gear—and sans everything from the cockpit to the wings.

Little old me? I managed pretty well. I mean, six guys were not a cakewalk, but they weren't a single sleepy astral fiend, either. I tripped up two guys and somersaulted over another pair, blasting energy between them as I spun upside down. My landing knocked the other two over. I threw a pulsar stave at a soldier, cracking off the top of his helmet, and whipped by fast enough to retrieve the weapon as it rebounded, then slapped both at the sides of another soldier.

They'd sent twelve guys out after us. Twelve unconscious and/or groaning guys were left.

Bruno's hatch popped open. He and Edith disembarked. Frank handed Ramos the M4 rifle from inside. "I'll take a stroll around the perimeter and see who else wants to play," Frank said. "Radio if you guys get stuck and need backup."

I glanced at Ramos, Edith, and Brandon, the last just now settling back to the ground. "Yeah, sure, if the four of us get in trouble, we might need the old guy and the robot."

"Good thing you're saying that now instead of when I had a medallion."

The hatch slammed shut and Bruno trundled into the woods.

"Okay, kids." I rolled a crick out of my neck. "Try not to break anything. It might come out of my paycheck."

We worked our way through the curved corridors, me following the painted markers leading to places like Liz's testing lab. I was buzzing with tension because we didn't encounter a single soul. Some of that was due to the pulsar stave humming in my hands. Either it was as wary as I was, or it was ready to knock back any symmachites that tried a second attempt at taking me over.

But the base was deserted. Security posts were unmanned. Labs were empty of personnel.

"If you can tap us into video surveillance, we can find where Xia and the others went," Ramos said.

I shook my head. "Not my area of expertise. What about a little inside, Edie—Edith?"

"The tachyon sensations are intense here, even without being in proximity to you two." Edie held up her hand. We were in the hall outside Tracking. I recognized the entrance but not the voices coming from inside. At least, until I heard a moderate-pitched voice crack, "Screw you!"

A *slap* resounded. Gravity flexed the air around me as Brandon made for the door, his face pinched with anger.

I caught him by the arm. "Easy. We can't barge in there, not without knowing the layout—the players. Let me talk to them. Sort things out. Then you guys can slam in and lock the situation down."

"Not with Sean involved," Brandon hissed. "He's gotten drawn into my battles one too many times."

"But you charging through the door isn't gonna make him any safer. Best case scenario, people will die." I blew out a breath. "I'll handle it."

Brandon scowled and stormed away. A door bent on its hinges.

I opened my mouth, ready to gift him with my trademark snark, but Ramos stood in my way. "Let him cool down. Brandon? Come back here."

Our superhero from the East Coast looked as baffled as I felt, but he obeyed.

"Mercury's right." Ramos jerked a thumb to the door. "If anyone can talk so much as to bluff his way through a standoff until we can get into place, it's him."

"Thanks. I think." I stuffed the pulsar staves into a pocket, where it was concealed but could still provide energy through the suit. "Ramos, wait for my signal."

"Keep it simple. I'm still rattled."

"Right." I glanced at Edie.

"I'll come with you." She holstered her bow. "And follow your lead."

My feet wouldn't move toward the door, no matter how much I tried talking myself into action. Sounded like a good plan. "You sure about that? I'm the new guy compared to you. No legacy to speak of—not on this world, anyway."

"That isn't true. Your family gave much to protect Earth and its people. I'm privy to many things, Mercury, some of which the upper echelons of Procyon doesn't want to share. They think they can hide accumulated secrets from a Pathkiller, like my forefather hadn't given his blood to turn back the tides of evil."

"I'm just trying to clean up this mess. There's nothing protective about it."

"Say that, and you might convince yourself. I'll have your back." Edie indicated Ramos, who was speaking with Brandon in a hushed conversation further down the corridor. "You can do what I haven't been able to—show yourself as the leader, rather than the shadow."

Talk about pressure. Confidence was never my problem. Fear that the confidence would lead to disaster? Near to crippling.

Come on, Mercury. They're counting on you. Everyone is.

I grit my teeth. Great. Move.

"Hey, Serena?" I hollered. "I'm home."

No one shot me as I entered Tracking. Someone

had found the switch for huge, blazing overhead lights. They threw into stark relief dozens of computer monitors and three huge screens at the front of the room. Several desks were arranged in semi-circles. Liz's array of consoles was in the direct center.

The seats were empty. Eighteen Procyon staff were clustered at the front, under the giant monitors. Liz was the beacon in the middle, pink hair glowing. The rest were techs I vaguely recognized, plus a handful of guys from Security in their black polo shirts. A few sported fresh bruises. No one seemed badly injured.

Between them and the door that was their escape route were the bad guys, for the moment: Serena Cyr, with Xia to her right. Teget was off to the left, Alvarez pinned in front of him by the ax. Dominic stood on the far right of the room, Echo Watches pulsing.

Sean knelt in front of Xia, red rising to his cheek where she must have smacked him.

"Hey, Mercury." Serena perched on the edge of a console. She smoothed her khakis. Guess her dress code shifted quick from elegant evening gown to Homeland Security business casual when the tables turned in her favor. "Thanks for stopping by."

"No problem, considering you broke into my place with my brainwashed buddies." I shrugged. "I'd ask what you want, but I'm not much for speeches, by either side. So, give me the sword, and nobody has to die."

"Sure. That's funny. I'll send your brother and your teammate to their demises first, then the rest of Procyon's loyal staff, long before I give it up. But I didn't want you to miss out on the show. See, the symmachites are another of those great presents the idiots of Meda provided. They were so obsessed with protecting everyone from the Interstice, they gave us the greatest tools to gain access to it."

She turned to Xia. "Kill him."

Xia raised the blade. Teget slashed with his ax at Alvarez.

Edie flung an arrow into its path, sending the ax off course enough that the weapon's sharp edges cut a bloody streak down Alvarez's chest. If she'd been a second slower, Teget would have slit the Procyon manager's throat.

Dominic flashed away, which left me no way to stop an opponent who could reappear at will.

I sped to Xia, the pulsar stave flashing as I attacked with the same ferocity I'd seen her use—mindless rage, except this was a mimicry. Identical moves, zero emotion.

No way I was gonna slide down that dark tunnel.

Ramos and Brandon stormed the room.

"There!" Edie pointed to a spot midway between her and them.

Brandon held up a palm.

Wind swirled around a pinprick of light as Dominic appeared, energy flashing from an Echo Watch. Edie leapt over Liz's desk, which absorbed the impact.

And Dominic toppled, Brandon's medallion-based

powers mashing him to the metal floor.

Ramos fired at Teget, who pushed Alvarez aside in order to avoid the incoming bullets. Alvarez clutched his chest where the ax had sliced into him. No one stopped Liz and Doctor Arne Becker from rushing to his side, which was good, because Doc Arne immediately did his best to staunch the flow of blood.

That gave the security guys a chance to rush Serena.

"Don't!" She produced a pistol and aimed it at the back of Sean's head. I didn't know much about the kind of gun, except the magazine jutting well below told me it was probably automatic and contained enough bullets to shred the kid. "Don't try it. I'm not here for anyone to interrupt. You'll have a role soon enough, as dinner."

A rumbling built in the room. Dust sifted from cracks in the concrete—dust that sifted sideways from the walls. Xia and I were locked together, stave pressed to blade, while Brandon kept Dominic pinned—no easy task, that, because Dominic blasted away at the invisible barrier, the Echo Watches letting streaks of light pierce it.

Ramos ducked behind a desk as Teget slashed through it, reducing it to metal fragments and glass shards. The computer sitting there blew apart. "A little help!"

"Here!" I threw half the pulsar stave.

Edie intercepted the stave, her jump carrying her across the room, and as she did, she fired an arrow.

It hurtled toward Teget.

He bashed the gun from Ramos' hand, severing the barrel clean off, and spun in time to snatch the arrow six inches from his face.

Except instead of miraculously seizing the arrowhead, he held the pulsar stave.

His cries echoed from the ceiling as a buzzing rose to meet the rumbling already in progress. Speaking of which, that rumble intensified so badly Xia and I broke apart, just so we could maintain our balance.

"Mercury!" Liz shouted. "Tachyon levels are spiking, and I don't think it has anything to do with the sword!"

"Half wrong!" Serena snapped. "The sword alone, no. But the sword and tiny new friends, just dripping witn Interstice energies? Let's say, my love is happy I've made it all come together."

Edie swung around, her bow steady, and fired at nothing.

Nothing, that is, until purple sparks coalesced around a deepening black gash in space-time. The gash rippled with swarms of symmachites, spewing from the sword. Tentacles with violet-tinged black hide lashed from its center, eight of them slapping at the metal floor and concrete walls. A mouth bulging with jagged fangs emerged.

The astral fiend screamed until the blazing arrow exploded deep in its gullet.

Everyone scattered, their cries filling the room. The shock of a rip opening up in the middle of

Procyon's primary control room was enough to worry anyone, but none of them—with the exception of maybe a few security guys—had seen one in person.

Neither had Xia.

I slammed the stave across her face, enough of a blow to send her sprawling, and finally got my hands on that stupid sword.

Teget fell sideways. His face was slack, arms trembling. He dropped the stave, but Ramos was there to catch it, and cradle Teget, too.

"Behind you!" Edie fired two more arrows.

She'd overestimated. Those shots exploded against the wall, too soon to intercept the rip that split the air and disgorged another astral fiend. It lunged for Ramos and Teget, not caring who was on whose side but only searching for a new meal with writhing tentacles. Those tentacles hammered nothingness a foot from Ramos' head.

"Get them back!" Sweat dripped down Brandon's nose. "I can't hold both!"

Both? I'd forgotten Dominic, who was still under the sway of the sword.

I aimed the weapon, swirling it in the same fashion as Xia, but Dominic still burst through the invisible barrier. The Echo Watches blazed at Brandon, who had to redirect his defenses. The sword wasn't working on him. What was I doing wrong?

Oh. I wasn't infected, that's why.

Edie leapt over a third rip that formed, sliding between a new pair of astral fiend tentacles. She brought an arrow down on the hide of the fiend trying to devour Ramos and Teget. It shrieked, the sound battering my ears, but that didn't stop her from ripping through the creature.

It screamed even more loudly, maw gaping, and she fired deep into its gullet. The fiend exploded in a misty spray of blue slime, the mess sublimating even as it spattered across the walls.

Among the chaos, I spotted Serena. She backed toward an empty rip, behind the third astral fiend that was menacing her set of hostages—while she dragged Sean with her. The kid kicked at her shins until she pressed that automatic pistol hard enough to his temple to draw blood. "Thanks for giving me another sneak peek of Procyon's operations!"

"No! Sean!" Brandon was backed into a corner, fending off blinding light from Dominic's assaults.

"He won't be in any danger from me," Serena said. "But where I'm going, I can't guarantee his safety. Between the Whisperer and Marigold Yen and my beloved Alex, there are many minds hoping you'll—"

The single gunshot sent her sprawling into the rip, her shout lost beneath the thunderous *crack*. Sean hit the metal, his sneakers scrabbling for purchase.

I vaulted the distance and grabbed his wrist.

The rips snapped and swirled until they sealed off in a reverberating *boom*. The third and final astral fiend lashed at everyone and everything in its grasp. Okay, Sean was safe, and Serena was gone. I could focus on—

Dominic screamed.

Edie had jabbed half the pulsar stave into his lower back. Telltale vibrations rid his body of the last of the symmachites, evaporating them with a golden glow.

His attention freed, Brandon whipped around, thrust out his fist, and reduced the final astral fiend into a pulpy, black and blue smear with a ripple of modified gravity.

Silence filled the room. A ragged set of cheers went up from the Procyon folks.

And as for the timely gunman—or I should say, gun*woman* …

Loredana walked through the open door, smoke rising from her MP5. "Doctor Becker, Miss Stojan, if Manager Alvarez is no longer in lethal danger, please escort him to the infirmary."

Everyone was in motion, not the least Brandon, who crushed his son in a tearful hug. I pushed past the security guys securing Xia and stood in front of Loredana. I lifted the mask. She swore blue jeans and a gaudy sweater, its design filled with imagery from the *Doctor Who* show done in red, white, and green, with snowflakes to boot.

"The ladies were understanding." Loredana smiled. "Though I would care to know more about the mechanical beast that met me at the parking garage."

"That was Bruno." I handed Loredana the sword.

She stared at the black sword.

"Anyway." I kissed her on the cheek. "Merry Christmas."

CHAPTER TWELVE

Ramos had to call in SCPD's special task force, because A.) we didn't have a private prison for the supervillains we defeated, and B.) no way we were inviting Homeland Security onto the premises of our new secret base.

Still satisfying to watch six guys wrapped head to toe in black body armor load Xia into a secure van.

"I'll have to turn her over to the feds," Ramos said. "I've already had to let a dozen calls go to voicemail. One from the mayor. Two from the governor."

The cops loaded into their vehicles and drove off, engine noises receding into the forest surrounding the base. "Nice. You gonna try for autographs?"

Ramos shook his head. Then he grimaced. "Remind me not to do that for a while."

"You'd better get Doc Arne to check you out."

"On my way now." He clapped my shoulder. "Nice work."

"Really? 'Nice work?' You've got to be joking." I chuckled. "Just took out my own allies, including a superhero with the capability of crushing us all in our sleep, and brought in a legendary forecaster from Procyon's oldest family line!"

"After letting her base of operations get destroyed."

"What? Hey. We had it covered."

"That isn't how I remembered it." Edie was standing to my left. I swore that spot was empty air a few seconds ago. "You cost me some of my favorite brass candleholders."

"Sorry." I scratched my neck. "In my defense, there wasn't a lot of time to train up on fighting superhero-turned-supervillain."

"Don't worry. It was time for change." Edie tilted her bow over one shoulder. She lifted her chin, as if feeling the breeze blowing across the tarmac of the makeshift landing pad. "I knew as soon as I got the call from Thomas."

Tyrone Thomas? That reminded me … I glanced at the bunker. Bruno the mech slumped on its hind legs, hatch wide open. "Any luck?"

Brandon climbed out. "Nothing. Not a scrap of paper."

"You seriously didn't expect Frank to stick around, did you? I mean, he is a wanted man."

"No, I understand. We just …" Brandon ran a hand through his hair. "We'd been through a lot. I'd hoped he was back in time to help for good. But not so much as a hint as to where he's been hiding out."

"Oh yeah?"

Sean climbed out behind Brandon. He shook his head and very emphatically mouthed, *No*.

"I bet he'll turn up," I said. "Seems like a reliable guy. Especially when you need someone to lend firepower."

Brandon's expression darkened as he and Sean walked over to us. "It's not a major deal, but … Never mind for now. Sean, we'd better get going."

"I know, Dad. Maybe check in with Doc Arne? See if you're like cleaned out of all the evil robot things?"

Brandon smiled and mussed his hair. "Not a bad thought. I'll be right back. And Mercury …" He offered a hand. "Thank you again for saving my son."

We shook. "Hey, I can only take so much credit. Loredana's the crack shot."

"Yes, but you led the team. You made the tough calls when things went sideways. That's no easy feat." He grinned. "I might even take notes."

I placed a hand to my chest. "Be still my heart!"

As soon as he ducked inside the bunker entrance, Sean glared at me.

"What gives?" I jerked a thumb. "I thought Frank was his Obi-wan."

"Yeah, okay, but Frank doesn't want Dad knowing where he's at." Sean shrugged. "Whatever. Something about finding his own way without interference."

"Is that why the Garrison didn't show up to either of these shindigs?"

"It's like Frank said. If they had come out, they would have killed him. And taken the medallion. Not what Dad wants."

"I bet death isn't on his checklist," I muttered.

"Sure." Sean scuffed at the dirt. He refused to make eye contact. "Okay, so, thanks for helping him out. And not killing him."

"You bet, kid. You're not a bad sidekick for Airfoil."

"That's *partner*."

Ramos chuckled as Sean hurried inside the bunker, presumably to check on his dad. "That is not unfamiliar."

"The attitude?" I snorted. "I bet, with the ages of your pre-teens and teen-ogre."

"Oh, I didn't mean them."

We headed into the base, weaving between Procyon staff busy with repairs. There were a lot of loose wires I hadn't noticed on our initial rampage. Smoke, too, but since no one was screaming about a fire or running around with extinguishers, I figured it was under control.

The infirmary was wall-to-crumbling concrete wall full of people, too, most of whom were sitting in rusty metal chairs with hideous puke green padding or laid out on beds. Brandon sat on the edge of one of those beds, arm extended, as a middle-aged Asian woman in scrubs drew blood. Sean had his face buried in his phone, shoe kicking against the wall. Kid looked so pale I was gonna asked him if he wanted smelling salts. My theory? Not a fan of the needles.

My favorite surly Millennial doctor was barking orders at people. I mean, if he were any more literally barking, I'd tell him to sit and stay. But his hair was slicked to perfection, and the beard groomed without so much as a millimeter out of place.

"If I wanted them sent out the door without a blood sample, I wouldn't have said *give me a blood sample from everybody*," he snapped at a tall, reedy young black man in medical scrubs. "Why don't you try that one more time before I send you to Elizabeth for target practice!"

"Doctor Becker." Loredana's voice cut across the tumult. Even dressed in her goofy Dr. Who sweater, with her arms folded she was every inch the operations boss. "We're all stressed. I would suggest you search for the mythical bedside manner I know you possess. The holidays are coming soon, after all."

"Humbug," Arne muttered, but he returned to checking on Alvarez's bandage without further whining.

"How're you holding up, Mister Manager?" I gave Alvarez a thumbs up.

"Well, considering my wound." Alvarez sighed. "Once again, we're in your debt."

"You're welcome. Also, how's that a bad thing? Because you act like we didn't win."

"I'm glad of that. But I'm worried you'll collect

on the debts you've accumulated."

I pantomimed shooting him. "You know it. And it'll involve copious amounts of vacation. Just remember to call me first when you've got a top-secret mission that involves evil weapons or sentient ancient robots. Because I'm the best."

Loredana rolled her eyes.

"Ever humble. Ms. Lark, if you'd take over things until I recover …"

"Gladly." She looped an arm through mine. "At least until our nuptials are resolved. Join me in the lab, my love."

"Yes, ma'am." I winked at Alvarez as we headed out the door.

Liz's testing lab was a cold, bare set of concrete walls and slab. A straight-up box. Wires ran in thick bundles across the ceiling and walls, like highways of electricity and data. A row of bright white lab coats hung by the door.

She and Dominic examined the black sword, which was suspended on hooks inside a container of transparent plastic. More wires ran from it into a bank of computer hard drives.

"Mercury!" Liz was a petite woman of Middle Eastern descent with a shock of pink hair and fire engine red Converse sneakers. She flung herself onto me, squeezing my ribs in a hug that was both heartwarming and injury-aggravating. "You made it!

Though I don't know why I sounded so surprised because you always make it through even when the odds are overwhelming which is crazy because there's so many enemies that get thrown—"

"Liz." I patted her back. "I'm okay. We're okay."

"Oh, good. Great!"

"Lordy, if that ain't the understatement of the decade." Wilhelmina, real name Sherry Jean Crown, strolled into the lab like she was on vacation. Which she must have been, because she wore flowery blouse of mingled pastel colors and a flowing coral blue skirt. She even had on flipflops, and her skin, the shade of rich mahogany, had gotten darker against the shock white hair.

She flipped up her sunglasses and patted my cheek, blue eyes shining. "Mornin', child.

"Hey, you." I checked my watch. Morning? Seriously? Yeah, it was well past midnight. Oof. "Checking in on everyone?"

"Only to make sure you ain't all been killed. Which it's nice to see hasn't happened."

"So sweet. Anyhoo …" I gestured to Liz. "What's the scoop on our latest razor sharp, uber powerful artifact?"

"It's made of the same Medan materials as the pulsar stave, the ax, and the night's blade, but combined in ways I haven't seen." Liz pulled up her report on her table—and by report, I meant a mishmash of data streams filling the screen. "Of course, there's a whole bunch of other alloys mixed in that I don't recognize. They're none we've seen before, either."

"She's convinced it has something to do with how Xia controlled the symmachites." Dominic prowled the periphery of the container. His face was drawn, pale, but he seemed to be recovering well. "There's evidence of circuitry at a microscopic level. Very advanced."

"How advanced?"

Dominic swung a device that looked like a gun, except it was a microscope mounted on gimbals. I peered into the other end. The lines along a chipped edge of the sword—the chip itself too small to be seen with the naked eye—were dazzling. "Those look kinda familiar."

"They should. I've gotten a peek at Airfoil's medallion." Liz's cheeks flushed. "I maybe kinda took a picture when he wasn't looking and enhanced it with Cyril. He was able to clean it up."

Sure enough, the image Liz offered next on her tablet was a fuzzy, smeared version of the same circuitry I'd seen through the microscope. "Wow."

"Indeed." Loredana took a turn with the microscope. "I shall endeavor to convince Manager Alvarez we need to question the individual called Xia about what she experienced under the influence of this weapon."

"Well, she hadn't absorbed any of the symmachites, if that's what you mean," Liz said.

"I understand. Nevertheless, she was able to

exercise control over our operatives and other individuals using direct mind-to-mind communication, with the symmachite microbes as the conduit. How the sword achieves it we have yet to determine."

"Any luck in the Historic Vaults?" Wilhelmina examined the tablet. She swiped through data until she found a magnified image of a symmachite. Think of a tick, except cybernetically modified and with way too many fangs. "'Cause this can't be the first time the symmachites have reared their nasty little heads."

"I … No. Not yet." Liz studied her shoes. "I mean, Cyril's running a search and I was hoping he'd get back to me—"

"Don't you worry none. I meant the older stuff, not what got scanned in." Wilhelmina pocketed her sunglasses and glanced at Loredana. "I hear these things were hiding in an ancient Greek pot. Might could be Procyon had a similar find a few decades back."

Loredana nodded. "I have a contact in Intelligence who might be of service."

As soon as Wilhelmina turned from the screen, Liz swiped back to where she liked them and relaxed.

"Bigger problem." I scratched my chin.

"Such as?"

"This thing's got no name. Nothing memorable." Loredana sighed.

"Robo-sword?" Dominic tried.

"Terrible," I muttered.

"Dark edge!" Liz offered.

"Better …"

"For goodness' sake," Loredana said. "Can we wait until it's property cataloged and investigated before bestowing a silly codename?"

Dominic covered his mouth with his hand. That didn't stop the chuckle from bleeding around his fingers.

"Don't worry," I told Liz. "She's just cranky because she got her party interrupted. And speaking of which …"

"Yes?"

I winked at Loredana. "I think we both deserve a Take Two."

Carlito's had plenty of seats open. It was Sunday afternoon, and we'd arrived after the post-church crowd had cleared out. The tinny music over the speakers and the scuff of shoes on tile floor were enough to set me at ease.

Having a much more relaxed version of our bachelor dinner was even better.

Our five were seated at a round corner table— "The booth of power," Teget deemed it as he slugged back a glass of pop.

I raised my glass. "To the best super-team a hero could hope for! Even if I did have to save all your butts."

Groans rippled around the table. Brandon flicked a mozzarella stick my way—unassisted by his fingers, of course. I caught it and devoured the weapon in one gulp.

"Don't forget to breath in between bites." Ramos clinked his glass against mine.

"Yes, sir, Lieutenant." I was glad we could get laughter back so fast after things had gone dark. But it was easy with these guys. Easier than I'd ever thought it could be, considering that nine months ago I was resigned to a solo life.

The things world-endangering threats will do to a person, am I right?

Dominic nudged Brandon. "Don't throw all our food. You promised Sean the leftovers."

"It's the least I could do after I abandoned him yet again," Brandon said. "No, not really. He's with his Uncle Reed—my friend. There's a new superhero movie they were both dying to see."

"What, and you ditched your kid for a delayed dinner with us?" I clucked my tongue. "I feel the need to chastise you."

"Don't bother. I can't stand those films. Sean knows it."

"You cannot stand tales of heroic adventures undertaken by beings who possess phenomenal gifts?" Teget chewed on his ice as if he were in the Sahara and he'd been given his first cold treat in days.

"Correct."

"There's an overabundance of irony there," Dominic said.

"I think it's fair to say none of us were planning

this journey as the way our lives would play out," Brandon said.

"But it's our path now," Ramos said. "There's no backing down from it. I know, I'm the cop, and there's a thing or two about duty I take for granted that you all could learn. That doesn't change our responsibility."

"To safeguard our worlds," Teget said. "And those beyond which may need our protection."

"Heavy stuff." I shook my head. "Let's keep our voices down so this doesn't wind up on Twitter."

"He's right, though. Both are." Dominic idly swirled a straw through his pop. "I could have lost everything if I'd been more blind to the threats facing us. Procyon gave me a chance to fix what I'd broken and give back more than I'd been given."

"Good deal." I gestured with a mozzarella stick—a half-eaten one. The pizza had better get here quick or I was gonna duel Teget for the last one in the basket. "As far as I'm concerned, the more allies we round up, the better."

"Glad you feel that way."

Man. I seriously was gonna check for an Echo Watch on Edie's wrist if she appeared behind me one more time. A smirk lurked at the corner of her mouth.

"Sorry, Edie, this is the boys' party. Girls are on the other side of the restaurant." I waggled my fingers in an exaggerated lovey fashion at Loredana, who sat with Liz and Wilhelmina against the far wall. She blew me a kiss. It wasn't her weekend away, but she said it would tide her over until her girlfriends could get back to town.

"I can tell by the rise in tachyon pulses as I approached the table." Her smirk unfolded into a grin. "And the increase in body odor."

"Burn," Brandon said.

"That sounded like your kid," Ramos murmured. "And mine."

They clinked their glasses together and poured more pop.

"I just wanted to congratulate you again on the victory and tell you I'm looking forward to having you fill out paperwork for me," Edie continued.

"I'msorrywhatnow?" The words spilled out.

"Loredana's offered me the Forecasting office here—at the San Camillo office." Light glinted off the wolf nose ring. "See you bright and early after the honeymoon."

I watched her walk back to the ladies' table. She said something to their gathering and all four burst out laughing.

"Is it too late," I asked the guys, "To request a transfer? Like, to Meda?"

"She is a great warrior, and a worthy ally," Teget said.

"Absolutely." I rubbed my forehead. "I'd just rather be eaten by an astral fiend than get paperwork."

CHAPTER THIRTEEN

Christmas Eve

Loredana and I got married twice.

Okay, that's an exaggeration. From a legal standpoint on this old Earth, we tied the knot at the courthouse downtown. The clerk signed our license in the presence of two witnesses: Teget, who insisted on wearing his traditional Medan garb of armored leather vest, knee-high boots, and loose-fitting tunic plus matching trousers; and a lady named Cordelia Keyes. She came dressed in a classy black skirt and jacket with a scarlet blouse. Her high cheekbones and coppery brown skin suggested West African descent. I recognized her from the texts Loredana sent me when I was in Paris with the guys.

Always nice to meet your wife's best friend five seconds before the wedding.

Right. So, the paperwork was signed. We were married.

I kissed Loredana. She looped her arms around my neck so we could better share the moment. Cordelia's restrained applause and Teget's shout of joy were dim background noise.

Of course, we made sure to put our names down—Mark Hale and Loredana Lark-Hale. Because, you know, "Mercury" wasn't a name anyone outside of Procyon knew. Even the average civilian hand toiling away in temporary offices on the legitimate charitable side of the foundation saw me—when they saw me at all—as "Mark."

"Lark-Hale's got a nice ring to it," I said. "Very *Star Wars*, Princess Leia."

"I don't follow."

"Expanded Universe. When she got married to Han? Organa-Solo. They had twins and—" I shook my head. "Never mind. It isn't even canon anymore."

"I shall take your word for it. But Lark-Hale fits."

"Congratulations." Cordelia's voice carried a hint of an accent. Could be Latino? She leaned in and kissed me on the cheek in a cool, professional manner just as similar.

"Thanks." I grinned. "And nice to meet you."

"Likewise. I hadn't pegged Lori for marrying any time soon, but then again, miracles happen at this time of year." Her smile hinted at mischief. "Bet we'll be seeing each other again, especially if your brother happens to accompany."

Teget was deep in discussion with a courthouse security guard who examined the ax's glittering blades with an expression approaching reverence. Glad Loredana had talked the staff into letting him take the thing past the metal detector. "Are we talking a social call or professional visit?"

"Either."

"Both would be welcome." Loredana hugged her friend. "Thank you again, Delia, for making the trip up to see us. I trust you'll remain for the reception?"

"I wouldn't miss it. Tell Archie to save me a dance. The rumba if he's still spry."

"Dad will trounce me if I don't."

"*Tu ya sabes.*"

I watched her leave. "Old pal?"

"We were at school together, yes. Harvard. Inseparable." She held my hand. "Delia's done consulting for Procyon, from time to time."

"Oh? What kind? Legal?"

"Private investigations, for our Intelligence division based in Miami."

Ah. One of these days I'd draw different conclusions based on first impressions.

My phone buzzed. Ramos. But, not a "You need to come stop this bad guy-slash-monster" call, thankfully. <The party's rounded up. We're all at Rosa Roja Park. Ho-ho-ho.>

<A Christmas joke? Ramos, you're slipping. Be there in 15.>

"Well, Mr. Hale." Loredana winked at me. "We are officially husband and wife."

"Yeah. It's funny—doesn't feel like it, does it?"

"Only because we have yet to exchange wedding bands." She admired the sapphire engagement ring

I'd given a few months ago. "The paper is simply that—paper that satisfies a legal requirement."

"But for our wedding … I know it's last minute, but are you sure you're okay with the officiant?"

She kissed me again. "I couldn't be happier."

I gotta hand it Dominic—he put in a lot of miles on the Echo Watches just to pull the real wedding off. I mean, transporting people and especially himself was part and parcel of his Procyon job. But a wedding party?

"Nice work," I murmured.

We gathered on the bridge along the Avenue of the West, over Meda's outermost canal. Ancient stone buildings surrounded us—smaller family residences, huge buildings with copper flashing and soaring domes, thick ivy dangling from all surfaces. A rickety wooden boat chugged north along the waterway, spewing steam as its occupants waved at us.

Our group faced my childhood home. It was a single story, made of white blocks with sandstone-colored columns at each corner. Hexagonal in shape. Copper dome. Ivy framed a wooden doorway with brass hinges at each corner.

Dozens of Medan citizens filled the streets nearby. Kids sat on parents' shoulders. I wasn't exactly a celebrity—didn't think Medans went in for that kind of thing. But Teget was a renowned warrior, and I was the one fated by my parents' death more than two decades ago to protect both dimensions. Our grandfather Naos had ruled the temple until his death; Teget assumed a great deal of responsibility splitting his time between there and Earth. So, they knew us.

It helped that a bunch were my cousins. I still hadn't figured how many.

I stood facing Loredana—me in a black tuxedo, right down to the bow tie. And, yes, I knew how to tie one, thanks very much. No clip-on for this guy.

She wore a gorgeous white gown, slim, elegant, without much adornment. But for me, she was just as beautiful when she'd shown up in the goofy *Dr. Who* sweater and jeans.

Our nearest and dearest were arrayed in a semi-circle toward us—Dominic, Brandon, Garvey from Procyon Security, Wilhelmina, and Liz, even Alvarez. No sign of Doc Arne; there was a nice bouquet of flowers at Loredana's condo in lieu of his appearance.

Archibald Lark, my new father-in-law, was at stiff attention behind Loredana. Poor guy had tears dripping onto his bright red moustache. He wasn't Procyon but given how much he'd learned about our true nature, there was no way I'd let him miss this.

Cordelia Keyes stood to Loredana's right. I guess her work for Intelligence ran a bit deeper than I realized.

Teget was at my right side. He held a black velvet box like it had nuclear launch codes nestled inside. Just two gold wedding bands. Grinning like a big dummy.

"Be bold, brother," he whispered. "Now is not a time for the faint of heart."

I winked at him and accepted the thinner of the two rings.

He reached for Loredana's hand and kissed her knuckles before giving her my ring. "And you, Lady Lark, I welcome to our household, in the line of Medan protectors."

Loredana's cheeks were aflame. "I … Thank you, Teget."

Ramos cleared his throat. He was somehow even more dashing than the rest of us guys in his black tux. He'd found creases to sharpen we didn't know existed. "I'm not an ordained minister, or whatever passes for a legal authority on this strange and wonderful world, but the bride and groom insisted on me performing this brief ceremony. So, I'll keep it simple.

"Mercury, you've always been a pain. I'm sure that will continue. But I've seen you grow into something more: A leader. There's a lot of responsibility piled onto your shoulders. A great deal the world—several worlds—expect of you. Let me make it clear: That's all secondary from now on." He touched Loredana's shoulder. "She's your highest priority. Make sure you never falter."

My heart hammered against my ribs which, thankfully, were healed up and no longer painful. "I will."

"Loredana, I've seen you handle everything. Even this kid." Ramos smiled. "Your patience and diligence balance his impulsiveness. I've never met a braver person."

She smiled back at him. "I have, Gabriel."

Ramos blushed. He lifted a well-worn Bible and read from it: "If I speak in the tongues of men and of angels, but have not love, I am a noisy gong or a clanging cymbal. And if I have prophetic powers, and understand all mysteries and all knowledge, and if I have all faith, so as to remove mountains, but have not love, I am nothing. If I give away all I have, and if I deliver up my body to be burned, but have not love, I gain nothing.

"Love is patient and kind; love does not envy or boast; it is not arrogant or rude. It does not insist on its own way; it is not irritable or resentful; it does not rejoice at wrongdoing but rejoices with the truth. Love bears all things, believes all things, hopes all things, endures all things.

"Love never ends. As for prophecies, they will pass away; as for tongues, they will cease; as for knowledge, it will pass away. For we know in part and we prophesy in part, but when the perfect comes, the partial will pass away. When I was a child, I spoke like a child, I thought like a child, I reasoned like a child. When I became a man, I gave up childish ways. For now, we see in a mirror dimly, but then face to face. Now I know in part; then I shall know fully, even as I have been fully known.

"So now faith, hope, and love abide, these three; but the greatest of these is love."

He closed the book, his eyes brimming with tears. Who am I kidding—the same went for me. Everybody was crying, at one level or another. Liz was flat out sobbing into Garvey's shoulder, who patted her shoulder gently.

"Mercury, Loredana, there are billions of people who have no idea the sacrifices you've made for them. But those who love you, the ones gathered here, they do. And more importantly, God knows. I pray His will finds you and keeps you. Seek Him, and He'll never let you go."

I was breathless. I could have been standing on the edge of a black hole, ready to dive in.

"Mercury, you're up."

Teget nudged me.

I blinked. *Focus*! My hand shook as I slipped the band onto Loredana's finger. "With this ring, I thee wed."

She did the same with my ring. Cold metal settled against the skin. "With this ring, I thee wed."

That was it. All we needed to say. No long vows or proclamations made before others; if they didn't know what we were about to do, well, they wouldn't be here.

I did offer up a silent prayer. *Thanks for bringing me here, out of a dark place.*

"By the power granted to me by the authorities of Meda and the wishes of my two friends, I now pronounce you husband and wife." Ramos grinned. "Go ahead and kiss."

The evening was full of more food and dancing and laughter than I'd ever experienced. Our reception being back on Earth, more people could show up—like Brandon's friend Reed Andreen, who had way too many questions for Dominic about the Echo Watches. That's how he arrived for the party, after all. But Dominic's wife Jessica dragged him free for a trip around the dance floor.

I sipped champagne and leaned back in a chair, my jacket discard, bow tie hanging loosely. Ramos swung by, his wife Olivia giggling as they followed the beat to—was Ramos doing the samba? Since when?

Archie Lark was in front of me, his moustache making him look extra dour. "Mercury."

"Sir."

"I suppose there's no undoing what's been done."

"I'll take that as a joke instead of an insult."

"Ta." Archie chuckled, though it wasn't as happy as I'd have liked it to sound. "Mayhap I've misjudged you."

"Mayhap? A tad."

"If you come back with 'cheery-O,' there will be no place I won't find you."

I didn't doubt it. "Look, Archie—"

"Stuff it. It's plain two me Lori is devoted to you—and from what I've seen, you're equally devoted to her. Do a tired old soldier a great courtesy and see to it that does not change."

"I promise."

He offered his hand, and we shook. Iron grip, but not bone-crushing. "Take care of my daughter, lad."

I nodded.

Thankfully, he was gone on his way deeper into the party and I could be alone again, for a few seconds. Nothing like your father-in-law warning you to be on your best behavior to set your pulse ticking up—especially when you'd seen him operate as a crack sniper against the forces of evil. Archie Lark might be a jerk, but I guess he was a jerk who was on my side. Which I could handle.

And if things were right between he and Loredana, well, all the better reason for me to give him a bit more respect.

Dominic slumped into the chair next to me. He wiped his brow with his sleeve. "I think this has me more worn out than the running battles we waged last week."

"No joke." I leaned back and closed my eyes, let the music carry deep into my core. "Hey, look, thanks for everything. Again."

"Such as?"

"Such as pulling our butts out of the proverbial frying pan more than once. And for … You know. Providing a sounding board."

"You're welcome. Everything good?"

"Are you kidding?" I took in the restaurant with

a sweep of my arms, as if I could gather up not just the people but the lights, the sounds, the smells, the sense of release and the feeling of joy at being able to be alive without fighting one terrible monstrosity after another and package it all forever. "I was an orphan. Now I have you guys."

Dominic nodded. He swirled his half-empty glass. "What I meant was, are you good in terms of being ready. For tonight."

My bleary brain thought he meant there was an astral fiend incursion scheduled, and I so did not want to tackle that later in the evening. But after he raised his eyebrows a couple of times, I realized he must have been super-subtly referring to our, ah, marital duties conversation. "I think so. I've tried not to stress."

"But have you talked about it."

"Sort of. In a roundabout way."

"Which is to say, not at all." Dominic sighed and shook his head.

"That's not what I said! We've—" I glanced at Loredana. She and Edith Pathkiller were laughing at a story Cordelia Keyes recounted, probably because her face was twisted into the goofy approximation of a circus clown. "Look. It's been an awkward subject."

"You're telling me."

"Then why do you keep harping on it?"

"I'm trying to be a good teammate, Mercury, and … I guess, a good friend."

Yeah. He really was. I could give him a break. I

grinned. "Tell you what: If you don't hear from me for a few days, assume we were just fine."

Dominic chuckled. "Cheers to that."

We clinked glasses.

Vigil Cove was a couple miles north along the coast, a dinky village I'd never paid any attention to. A lone lighthouse with a black top and candy cane striping slumped on a heap of rocks perched at a bowl-shaped harbor. Signs warned of ongoing renovation. Other than that, the only thing Vigil Cove had going for it was the cars bunched around six or seven restaurants and a couple bed-and-breakfasts.

Loredana and I rented a solo cabin.

I'd give you a full description of its décor and architectural provenance, but we were—otherwise occupied.

When we did finally surface from kissing for air, Loredana's breaths came out feathery. "Well."

I nodded, equally winded. "Yeah."

A light drizzle was subsiding, the moisture clinging to our hair—until it shifted to chunky flakes of snow. One landed on the tip of my nose. I went cross-eyed.

Loredana laughed. She brushed it free. "I would ask again, but I feel as if we've been over the subject innumerable times."

I snorted. "Pretty much. You okay?"

"I am. Yes." Her cheeks, already flush from champagne and dancing, went deeper scarlet.

"Though I must admit, I never would have dreamed such apprehension from the least dangerous situation I've been in for months."

"I hear you. But hey …" I took her hands. "Us. Together. Right?"

"Yes. Together." She opened the door and led me inside. "Always."

Fun fact: You can undo a lot of buttons without looking where your hands are if you're motivated, in a marital sense. I reached for the door, missed the handle twice before I could swing it shut. Then swung it open again to make sure the "Do Not Disturb" sign was facing the right way.

As for what happened next, well, that's none of anybody's business.

Fade to black.

Mercury's adventures continue...

Stay tuned

www.steverzasa.com

www.ingramcontent.com/pod-product-compliance
Lightning Source LLC
Chambersburg PA
CBHW061216210726
48294CB00006B/1856